LUKE'S OBSESSION

RED LODGE BEARS - BOOK ONE

KAYLA GABRIEL

ONE

You Are Cordially Invited...

The Beran Family is proud to be hosting a social mixer at 5 p.m. on June 4th, 2014 in Red Lodge, Montana. The event will feature live music and food, complete with instruction on how to two-step! All eligible Berserkers from Alpha-blooded families in any clan are encouraged to attend. Bring your cowboy boots and come dance the night away!

*A*ubrey Umbridge stared down at the pristine piece of white card stock held loosely in her fingers, confused.

"An invitation..." she said, her brow furrowing as she looked up at her parents. The living room of her family home seemed smaller somehow, as if the chair she occupied was several feet closer to the couch where her parents sat than it had been a few minutes before. The idea of a social mixer with other mateable Berserkers made her mouth go dry, her pulse speed up… and not in a good way.

"Yeah," grunted her father, never much of a talker. He was six foot six of pure, burly Alpha bear, all capped with a head bright silver hair and a perpetual scowl.

"This is what you summoned me out of the city for? I told you guys that I have a really busy week working at the shelter," Aubrey said, cocking her head.

Aubrey's mother leaned forward, and for a moment Aubrey was reminded where she'd got her own looks. Aubrey's mother was five foot five, built with nothing but curves. Her round, sweet face and sparkling green eyes were a perfect mirror of Aubrey's own; only her mother's age and short, light brown hair differentiated them. Aubrey's own hair was waist-length and dyed a deep cherry red, framing her plus-sized body to perfection and making her dark clothes and pale skin stand out.

"Aubrey," her mother said. "We… it's important that you attend."

Aubrey glanced at the invitation again, perplexed.

"It's this weekend! I can't go to this, I have a movie date with Valerie and Samantha," Aubrey protested.

"Well, dear—" her mother began.

"It's mandatory," her father cut in.

Aubrey's jaw dropped.

"Excuse me?" she managed after a moment.

"Required. Not optional," her father said.

"I— I know what the word mandatory means, Dad!" Aubrey cried. "I'm more concerned about why you think you can force me to attend some... some shitty Berserker social function. Why in the world would you want me to do that, and why would I ever agree?"

"To find a mate," her father said, leaning back against the couch and crossing his arms. "And you need to watch that language in this house."

Aubrey found herself speechless for the second time in as many minutes.

"To find a mate?? You have got to be kidding me! What makes you think you can just demand that of me?"

"Now Aubrey, dear," her mother said, trying to mediate. "It's not just you. It's all the children of Alpha families."

"Dad's not Alpha anymore," Aubrey pointed out. "He retired two years ago. I don't even qualify for this... this *invitation*."

"I was part of the Alpha committee that decided on this. The discussion started years ago," her father said.

Aubrey looked at him for a long moment, trying to understand what was going on.

"The Alphas' council has nothing better to do than arrange speed dating events for their kids? I have trouble believing that."

"Well, you'd better suspend that disbelief, Aubrey. The council isn't going to sit around and watch our kind die out just because your generation doesn't want to settle down. This event is not a choice. Finding a mate in the next year is mandatory for all single Berserkers from twenty one to forty five. No exceptions," her dad said.

"Are you listening to yourself? This sounds an awful lot like the talk you gave me before you pushed me on Lawrence."

Aubrey didn't miss the way her father flinched at the man's name.

"This isn't the same," he defended.

"Aubrey," her mother interceded. "This isn't something new. Berserkers have always done this in times of hardship. It's how your father and I met, if you'll remember."

"You made me a promise! Or have you forgotten?" Aubrey challenged them.

Her father rose to his feet, his face growing red with fury.

"It's been two years, Aubrey! I would have given you anything back then, anything to make you feel safe again. But I never thought you'd be alone for almost a decade. You haven't had a single serious boyfriend since then, and that's just not going to fly anymore."

"I've had boyfriends," Aubrey said, stung.

"Bears?" her father asked, raising a brow as he moved toward her, growing aggressive. His bear was close to the surface, rising as surely as his temper. Aubrey's bear was right behind his, pushing at her in a bid to be free. The bear protected Aubrey savagely at every turn, and wasn't about to let a little thing like a towering Alpha male get in the way of that duty.

As she tried to keep her bear at bay, a sneaky thought popped into her head. Normally Aubrey would do anything to avoid seeing her father slip into a rage, but at this moment it would provide her a little leeway. If he shifted and started destroying furniture, her mother would shift in order to quell him. Aubrey would be forgotten in the melee, and she'd be on her way back to San Francisco before they even realized she was gone. She just needed to push him a little further, and her father would snap.

"What does it matter who I date?" Aubrey hissed, standing and staring her father in the eyes.

Her mother interceded, grabbing her father's wrist and tugging him back a step. Her mother turned on Aubrey in the next moment, easily guessing what Aubrey was doing.

"Because you're a pure bred Berserker, and you have a duty to pass those genes along, Aubrey Rose Umbridge. Now stop trying to pick a fight with your father."

"I'm not taking a mate," Aubrey said, crossing her arms to mirror her dad's pose.

"Then you'll be banned from the clan, and I know you don't want that," her mother said.

"You— you're not serious!" Aubrey exclaimed.

"Look, I know this isn't something you want. You

have your life in the city, and your friends. Your father and I are glad that you've found your way, we really are," her mother said.

"But?" Aubrey prompted.

"But you have to try to find a mate. It's not something that we sought out, but it's happening. All we're asking for right now is that you attend a party, which isn't a very big deal, is it?" her mother asked.

"A party in Montana, where I have to choose some strange man to take as a life partner. I will repeat myself; are you kidding me?"

"You're going," her father said, shaking his head and retreating to stand near the couch. "We're not going to discuss this any further. Will you need to be escorted to the mixer, or will you attend on your own?"

"Jack! Quit being a bully, you're not helping!" her mother sighed. "Aubrey, please. Please just go to the party. Stay for an hour, meet a few people. If you hate it, we'll try another tack."

Looking at her mother's worried face, Aubrey melted a little.

"Fine," she sighed. "I'll go, but this isn't going to work. I like my life the way it is. I'm not meant to have a mate."

"Stubborn," her father muttered, turning and stomping off toward his man-cave shed in the back yard.

"Thank you, dear. I think if you give it a chance, you might even have a good time," her mother offered.

"Right. Well, if that's the last of the insane demands for today, I'm going to head home," Aubrey said.

Aubrey saw the hurt in her mother's expression as she left, but she couldn't bring herself to soothe it away. This was only the latest in a long line of demands from her father, broken promises made in the name of saving the Berserkers. This was America, not some backward third-world country, and yet her kind were still subject to the same social pressures and marital arrangements as Indian brides.

Seething, Aubrey climbed into her black VW rabbit and navigated her car onto the highway. I-5 passed by as she worked through the problem in her mind, the scene outside her windshield becoming a blur of white-dotted lines in the growing darkness.

For about the thousandth time, Aubrey wished she'd been born human. If she had, none of this would be happening. Even the thing with Lawrence wouldn't have happened.

She shuddered and forced her thoughts away from that bleak period of her life. Her mind drifted to the party, to the thought of eligible men. She had to admit that she wouldn't mind meeting a hunky stranger and having a little private tete-a-tete, but she didn't want more than that. It had been far too long since she'd had wild, heart-racing, breath-stealing sex.

She sucked in a breath, unable to stop her mind from going straight to Luke. Luke, her every fantasy come to life. Luke, the no-last-name lover. The

Berserker who'd shared the one moment in her adult life where Aubrey had solidly fucked things up all on her own. It was her biggest moment of regret, bigger even than agreeing to meet Lawrence for the first time.

Luke… She'd met him during a weekend getaway in San Diego. It was almost two years ago, though Aubrey could barely believe that. Luke was incredible, good enough to skip out on the whole weekend of fun she'd planned with her college girlfriends. She'd met him in the bar of her hotel, both recognizing each other as Berserker blood. Luke had been so tall and muscular, his dark hair clipped short, his jawline dusted with several days' worth of stubble. And those eyes… he had the most incredible eyes, like dark sea glass. He'd introduced himself, asked her name, and twenty minutes later they were in the gilded hotel elevator, lip-locked and panting for more.

They'd laid in his hotel bed together for forty-five solid hours, laughing and ordering room service champagne and exploring each other's bodies. The sex was mind-altering, truly like some kind of drug. He'd touched her everywhere. Though he was the silent type, he kept up a running commentary of compliments and pleas and soft growls, all while his big hands swept over her hips and thighs and arms and stomach, the places on her body that made her feel insecure. He was insatiable, every bit as hungry for her as she'd been for him. The time they spent together was a balm to her soul, healing some of the dark, broken places inside her that Lawrence had twisted up and charred.

And yet, she'd never asked his last name. When Luke kissed her for the last time, eyes growing dark as he explained that he was redeploying the next day and had no choice but to leave, Aubrey made a decision. She wanted their time to stay perfect, a crisp bubble of memory that she could hold onto.

So she'd just given Luke a hug and thanked him. When he got up to take a shower and dress, she'd packed up her bag and fled. She hadn't even let herself try to find him, though she'd thought about him nonstop for over a year. She could never quite let the idea of him go, even though he made her think of…

She shut the thought down. Now was no time to be thinking of her deepest, darkest secret, something she could barely even admit to herself.

No, she'd rather think of Luke, how sexy he'd been. He was still her favorite fantasy; any time she got lonely and decided to take the edge off with a little self-love, Luke was there for her.

Aubrey shifted in her seat, realizing that tonight was shaping up to be one of those nights. Something to get her mind off the weekend, at least. Turning up the radio, she smiled to herself and pressed on the gas, marveling as the San Francisco skyline loomed up ahead.

TWO

*A*ubrey stood in the oversized guest bathroom at the Montana Lodge, staring at herself in the mirror. Her long hair was twisted into a loose side braid, mascara rimming her bright green eyes, a little blush bringing out her cheekbones. She wore a delicate, empire-waisted dress just the creamy yellow color of afternoon sunlight, the neckline dipping to show off her décolletage. A pretty white lace ribbon circled her waist just below her generous breasts and tied at her back, shaping out the hourglass of her figure. She'd finished her ensemble with a soft, short-sleeved white cardigan and fire-red cowboy boots, a beloved impulse purchase she'd made a few years back and rarely had the opportunity to show off.

She looked down at her arms, at her tattoos. She had a thick black ankh on one wrist, and a Celtic wrought-iron cross on the other. One of her upper arms featured a beautiful grass-green snake coiled around a vivid red apple. The other arm had a scattered pattern of tiny stars, moons, and planets in different colors. She loved her tattoos, and added one to her collection every year as a birthday present to herself.

Turning to the side, Aubrey sighed. The party outside was in full swing, and here she was hiding in the freaking bathroom. She'd had a couple of cocktails, danced a few turns with a couple of handsome Berserkers, and still she felt... frumpy. No matter how well dressed she was, how witty her banter could be, her heart just wasn't in it. She kept looking around at her competition, noticing how a few of the Berserker females were modelesque blondes who flirted and mingled with ease.

Aubrey was more than a little full-figured. She had big boobs, wide hips, and a seriously serious ass. Biting her lip, she looked at her phone. She only had to make it for another twenty minutes, and then the reluctant promise she'd made to her mother would be fulfilled.

Is it really trying if you hid in the bathroom for half the party? she chided herself.

Straightening, pushing back her shoulders, she forced herself to leave the bathroom and head back outside. When she stepped out onto the Lodge's wrap-around porch, fiddle music swelled and engulfed her. She decided she'd get another drink first, and then give socializing one more try. Maybe after that she could even find that cute dark-haired guy she'd danced with before and take another shot at the two-step.

She stepped down into the buzzing crowd, only making it a few feet before a huge blond guy staggered backward and almost knocked her down.

"You're such a fucking waste of space, Emmet!" another man shouted.

Aubrey peered around the blond man to find a handsome dark-haired Berserker, face flushed red with fury, fists clenched against the need to shift and fight. She eyed the guy, thinking he looked a little familiar. Then again, she'd thought that about four different times tonight. She kept seeing these tall, dark, and handsome types and thinking that they reminded her of Luke.

Luke isn't here. He's a fucking catch, of course he's already mated. Stop being so pathetic, she reminded herself for the fifth time.

The blond guy said something nasty, and the dark-haired guy moved like lightning. His fist connected with the other Berserker's face, blood welling instantly. Aubrey made a face and shuffled out of their way, letting the sea of strangers pour in and break up the fight before things got out of hand.

Aubrey made a wide loop around the outside of the tent in order to avoid all the fuss. She just wandered and people-watched for a minute, then remembered that she'd been headed for the bar. Making a beeline for her next vodka cranberry cocktail, she stopped behind a drunk couple who were taking up multiple seats at the bar. From the way the blonde was draped over the big guy's body, it seemed like the mixer was working out just fine for them.

She stepped right up behind them, feeling silly as she waved to the bartender, trying to get his attention.

"Water. Lots of water," the man at the bar mumbled when the bartender arrived.

Aubrey froze. That voice… she knew that voice. For a split second, she was afraid that she'd somehow ended up standing right behind Lawrence. But he wouldn't be here, of course. He had a mate and lived on the other side of the country.

And then it hit her, the reason she knew that gruff voice. It had played in her very naughty fantasy, only days before. Unfortunately, rather than making her tingle all over like his voice did in her dreams, in person it made her blanch.

It was Luke, of all fucking people. He was here, all right. And halfway wearing a thin, drunk blonde girl whose hand was creeping up his thigh, heading straight for his cock. Something dark stirred within her, a flash of guilt, shame, and fear all at once. Anger, too, though she didn't understand that reaction at all.

Luke stiffened, sensing the holes she was burning in his back. Before Aubrey could turn and run, he turned and made direct, close eye contact. His expression was puzzled for a moment before it fell, as if he couldn't be less thrilled to see her.

"Aubrey!" he exclaimed. She couldn't help but gape at him for a second, all that tall, dark, and handsome suddenly just inches from her fingertips. And in a compromising position with another lady, no less. Aubrey eyed the woman without malice; she just hoped the other woman would be smarter than she herself had been. Much more careful.

"Luke," Aubrey replied, making a point to look away from the blonde that was now scooting herself into his lap. Her gaze was drawn back to him in a mere moment. Aubrey couldn't help notice that his hair was longer now, less soldierly. His tan was lighter, too, but he was every bit as gorgeous as when she'd first laid eyes on him. Looking at him made her heart wrench in a way she hadn't felt since the moment she'd walked away from him two years ago.

"Uh… this isn't what it looks like. I'm drunk," he said, pushing the woman back into her own seat.

Aubrey was surprised for a moment, since Luke had made a big point out of not drinking when she'd met him. Then she realized that it didn't matter. This whole interaction was ridiculous, and she wanted nothing more than to escape. She'd done her duty to her parents, and now it was high time that she headed home. There was absolutely nothing here for her but heartbreak.

"I see," she said. "Of course."

She turned to leave, but Luke lurched forward and grabbed her wrist. His eyes dropped down to her cleavage, then darted over to her tattoos, mostly new in the years since she'd seen him. Something about the way he looked at her made her skin draw tight, and she shivered.

"Aubrey, wait!" he insisted.

"I think not," she snapped, trying to pull from his grasp.

"I didn't know you'd be here!" he said.

"Yeah, me either. Now let me go," she said. Ripping away from him, she whirled and half-ran from the tent.

Her eyes stung with hot tears, shame and anger filling her once more. She scolded herself inwardly. Luke was nothing to her, she was nothing to him. Just a two-night stand from years ago. What right did she have to feel like this?

Before she could try to parse any of the hurt and fury flooding into her chest, she was already in her rental car, pulling out of the Berans' driveway.

"No. Never again," she promised herself. "And don't you dare cry."

Revving the engine, Aubrey took herself as far away from Luke as she possibly could.

THREE

*L*uke Beran sprawled on the queen-sized bed in his hotel room, bleary-eyed from lack of sleep.

After running into Aubrey in the worst possible circumstances, he knew he'd make a terrible mistake.

"Fubar'd," he muttered aloud. "Fucked it up beyond all repair, for sure."

And yet, Luke was still trying to fix things. After Aubrey had fled the party, Luke made the decision to locate her and apologize. Maybe if he did a good enough job, Aubrey might forgive him. And if he pulled out all the stops and charmed the shit out of her, maybe she'd consider more than forgiveness. She might, say, come back to his hotel room and rock his world like she had the last time.

"You fucking wish, asshole," he groaned to himself.

He was running on pure luck and brain fumes at

this point. If he wasn't such a curious fucker to begin with, something that usually got him shit tons of trouble, he wouldn't even have Aubrey's full name. When they'd spent that weekend together in San Diego in 2012, he'd been half in love with her and hadn't even known it. What a blow it had been to get out of the shower, planning just what he'd say to convince her to give him a shot, how he'd ask her to wait for him to come back from his latest deployment.

How the hell could Luke track down and beg her for more than a lost weekend when he didn't even know her last name?

As he'd dragged his sorry ass through the lobby, a thundercloud of rejection hanging over his head, he'd stopped at the checkout desk. Staring at the clerk, he realized that she'd been a guest at the same hotel. Luke had bullied, bribed, and begged every person at the front desk until they'd given him the five words he so needed: Aubrey Umbridge, San Francisco, California.

After that, he'd wheedled one of the more technology-inclined members of his unit into helping him use social media to find out all he could about Ms. Aubrey Rose Umbridge. He'd watched her from afar, even saving a few of her low-res public Facebook photos to his laptop. He'd lay in his bunk every night, dreaming about getting some furlough so he could go track her down and ask her out again. Maybe get another taste of Aubrey's lips, touch her bountiful, pale-skinned curves.

And then shit had gone sideways. After the initial

Arab Spring uprisings, the Army brass had transferred Luke's unit had been transferred to Jordan to deal with the overflow of the Syrian civil war. After a decade of service in Afghanistan and Iraq, the transition was difficult. New languages, new culture, new problems. Half their unit personnel had changed too, which meant losing contact with some of his closest and oldest friends.

Just when Luke was settling in, an overtaxed and mentally ill private had lost his shit and shot up their own camp, killing three of Luke's close friends and a dozen others. Luke was the one who took the twenty-year-old private down, out of the sheer shitty luck of being in the same room and having a weapon at hand.

For a long time after that, Luke hadn't thought about much more than trying to live out the rest of his deployment without getting his ass blown up by someone, whether enemy or friend. He hadn't forgotten Aubrey, not by a long shot, but he'd gone into a kind of mental hibernation, just focusing on survival.

So he'd done his time and left the Army behind. He'd returned to the States, and though Luke knew he was a hell of a lot safer, he didn't feel any better. He was like a fish out of water here, and it had been a rough time.

Then he'd seen Aubrey. She looked just the same, that sweet face and fiery dark red hair, those luscious curves. His body had hardened even as his heart had flip-flopped in his chest, and for a moment he genuinely felt... hope. For the first time since he'd come home... Hell, since he'd shot that kid down in Jordan, really, he'd felt like things might turn around for him.

Aubrey had took one look at his drunk ass and the girl in his lap, who'd already promised to suck his dick later, and she'd turned tail and ran. Luke couldn't blame her, not one bit. That didn't mean that he was letting her go, though, not really.

Luke snapped out of his reminiscence when a car alarm went off somewhere outside his second-story hotel room. His whole body tensed, and he broke out into a fine sheen of sweat all over his body. He lay still for a couple of minutes, forcing himself to breathe deep when all he wanted to do was abandon ship. Car alarms had been a big signal of coming violence in Jordan, and their sound still chilled his blood, made him antsy.

One of the things he found hardest in his post-Army life was the task of being still; in the service, there was always something to be done. If you weren't racked out for the night, you had a long list of shit that needed doing. He liked to stay busy, because a moving target is safer than a sitting duck. Here, though, every-thing was waiting rooms, sitting areas, long lines, and people with infinite patience all standing around. Just standing, sipping their Starbucks, waiting for life to happen.

Luke hated it.

He released the breath he'd been holding, telling himself that he needed to sleep. Really, actually sleep, not just lay in his darkened hotel room with all his clothes on in case… He shut the thought down before it started to get crazy. Nothing was going to happen, he was just exhausted.

The last few days had been a whirlwind of long car trips, plane flights, waiting in airports, and many terse conversations with his old unit commander Stephen Collinswood. Stephen had retired before the unit got transferred to Jordan, and he was now living in Seattle with his wife and two kids. Stephen was one of the few friends Luke had that was both alive and not still enlisted. He was also a wolf shifter, which meant he understood some of Luke's weird civilian life issues. Therefore, Stephen was Luke's defacto confidante.

Stephen also worked for the Seattle Police Department, which meant that when Luke had decided to track down Aubrey, Stephen was Luke's first phone call. Stephen took pity on him and given up her Alpha's information, though he'd refused to hand over anything personal like her address.

The day before, Luke had been out at her Alpha's house, with mixed results. James Erikson wasn't the most friendly Berserker on the planet. In fact, he reminded Luke of his own father. Luke had laid out his attempts to locate Aubrey, promised that he had the best of intentions, even given his father and Stephen's names and phone numbers as references. Erikson was closemouthed and skeptical, despite apparently having agreed to the whole forced-mateship issue.

Just as Luke was about to cut his losses and try something else, Erikson had said that he thought Aubrey worked at "some homeless shelter, some women's rights bullshit".

At least it gave Luke a place to start. He clambered out of the bed and toed off his shoes, then stripped down to his boxers. One of the most amazing things about being stateside was the ability to sleep mostly nude, and he tried to take advantage of it. Well, on the nights where he felt calm enough to undress at all, that was.

Turning off the light on the night stand, he splayed out on his back and stared up at the ceiling. His mind drifted back to Aubrey. She'd looked so hot the other night, all done up like that. She'd been dressed very innocently, and damn if it didn't make him wonder what she had on underneath. When he'd stripped her back in San Diego, she'd worn this sexy red bra and lacy black panties.

He shifted on the bed, his hand wandering down to rest on top of his hardening erection. Luke closed his eyes and remembered the way she'd shivered when he'd peeled off her dress, more from excitement than the cool air against her skin. And her skin…

Aubrey was nothing but amazing, unblemished

peaches and cream from head to fire-engine-red-tipped toes. Luke liked women in every shape and size, but he especially liked a woman with curves like Aubrey's. Some guys talked shit about bigger girls, but Luke liked a nice, plump ass and big tits, liked a woman that he could spread out and fuck hard.

Thinking about that, picturing her naked and ready for him, Luke pushed his boxers down his hips and took his cock in his hand. He was already so horny that a single pump of his fist made him suck in a deep breath, his cock twitching under his fingers. He was going to have to temper himself a little bit now, if he wanted to last more than half a minute. Thinking about his girl, though... She'd been so perfect, driving him crazy.

With Aubrey, he hadn't felt the slightest need to hold back. When he'd got her out of her dress, he'd pulled her tight against his body and kissed her hard, testing her. She was so sensitive, responding to every flick of his tongue against hers, every movement of his hands over her hips and sides. But she'd given as good as she got, scraping her nails over his scalp and shoulders, nipping at his bottom lip, moaning into his mouth when he'd slipped his hand down and brushed his fingers over the front of her panties.

When Luke thought about touching her hot, wet slit for the first time, he groaned. He'd laid her back on the bed and stripped her bare, cupping those big tits of hers in his hand, biting, licking, and sucking her petal-pink nipples until she was rocking her hips and panting for breath. Then he'd pressed her knees apart and teased her, touching her hip bones, her inner thighs, and her mound. By the time he'd run a single fingertip up and down her pink folds, she'd been so wet for him.

Luke pumped his fist faster and harder, feeling his balls tighten up.

He fast-forwarded the moment in his mind, thinking of when he'd had her on her hands and knees, spread and ready to take him deep. He'd plunged into her channel, the tight heat gripping him like the finest glove. Just like now, he'd been forced to keep himself in check, to rein in the orgasm threatening to overtake his body.

Then she'd started talking to him, encouraging him.

"Fuck me, Luke," she'd panted. "Yeah, take me just like that, right there. Oh god, make me cum, Luke!"

And then she had, clamping down on his cock as she screamed his name…

Luke lost control of the moment, bowing up off the bed as he came. He pulsed his seed into his hand, crying out as he pictured Aubrey taking his cock, covering him with her hot cream, begging for more. At last he collapsed, shaking, struggling to breathe.

It took him a full minute to get up and wash himself off. He glared at the bed before climbing back in, realizing that thinking about his time with Aubrey had made him feel less alone for a few minutes. Now, of course, it was back in full force.

Wrapping himself in the comforter, Luke closed his eyes and forced himself to relax, to let sleep overtake him. His last thought was that one day soon, he might not be sleeping alone anymore.

FOUR

Luke pulled his black rental sedan up to the curb on Mission Ave. in the quiet downtown area of Sunnyside, California. He checked the piece of paper sitting on his passenger seat, making sure address scrawled across it was correct. Checking out the numbers on each side of the street, he soon spotted a squat, drab brick building halfway down the block. There was nothing on the outside to indicate the contents, except a small bronze plaque bearing the address. One last glance at the piece of paper affirmed that the building was indeed the Sunnyside Women's Center, Aubrey's current place of employment.

Behind the boring brick was a top secret women's shelter and resource center for victims of violence and domestic abuse. While the trail of breadcrumbs leading to the shelter had been few and far apart, Luke had found Aubrey's name on the list for a number of charity events, and never as a patron. The realization that she might be working for a non-profit rang true to Luke's memories of Aubrey.When he'd been with her back in San Diego, she'd mentioned wanting to do more for her community, specifically for women trapped in unsafe homes.

Luke followed the trail, finding several shelters who were beneficiaries of the galas and auctions Aubrey had attended, cross-matching charity names with shelter locations. Luke had spent the morning narrowing down the list of possibilities, then calling and trying to get an appointment with Aubrey at all the places on his list. Women's shelters had crazy tight security, so the going was tough, but one secretary had slipped up and responded to Aubrey's name.

Now he stood outside the Sunnyside Women's Center, hoping he wasn't going about things all wrong. Before he could chicken out, Luke stepped up to the steel-reinforced security door. When pulling the handle revealed that the door was locked tight, he pressed an unmarked buzzer on the right side of the door frame. There was a mechanical whirring sound, and Luke looked straight up into a set of security cameras that swiveled his way. He stepped back and kept his face tilted upward, trying not to look menacing. It was hard to look innocuous when you were over six and a half feet tall with dark hair and a full beard. Bear shifters didn't come in smaller sizes, nor did they generally walk around with dazzling grins.

He must have passed the inspection, because after a moment the door buzzed and the locks clicked open. He pulled the door open and entered a white-tiled room where two more security doors flanked a reception desk behind bulletproof glass. He stepped up to the glass, leaning down to peer at the young blond girl who stared back at him. She reached out and pressed an intercom button before speaking.

"Can I help you?" came the tinny sound of her voice.

He leaned down toward the speaker on his side and pressed the button.

"Uh, yeah. I called about making an appointment with Aubrey Umbridge," he said.

The girl gave him a long look, then shook her head.

"I'm sorry, I don't know that I can help you."

"Can you ask Aubrey to come up? She'll want to see me," Luke said. He kept his face smooth and blank, hoping not to scare the girl into raising the alarm. He wasn't here to hurt or scare anyone, but he wasn't exactly here with Aubrey's approval, either.

The girl pressed the intercom button again.

"I'm sorry, I can't help you. I'm going to have to ask you to leave," she said.

"Ma'am, I promise you that Aubrey knows me. I'm only here to see her. We, uh, we're friends," he said, giving her a look that intimated a very personal situation.

"I can't—" the girl started the same rote recitation

again, but then a door in the office opened and Aubrey walked in. The young blonde turned around, eyes growing as big as dinner plates. Aubrey's mouth opened, probably a greeting of some sort, but it only took seconds for Aubrey's gaze to snap upward.

The way her eyes narrowed and mouth thinned made Luke think she was even less pleased to see him than he'd suspected. Aubrey looked back at the younger woman, giving her a reassuring smile and a pat on the shoulder. The blonde stood and gave Luke one last suspicious glance before vacating the office.

Aubrey stalked up to the window and leaned down to the intercom, the dark red curtain of her hair swirling around her curvy frame as she reached out and pressed the intercom button with a single scarlet-tipped fingernail.

"What are you doing here?" she asked, her emerald eyes snapping with emotion.

Luke stepped forward, his lips turning up at the mere closeness of her. He pressed the intercom and leaned down.

"I'm here to see you," he said.

She scowled and leaned forward again, her low-cut black cotton dress giving him a glimpse of creamy, bountiful cleavage. Luke looked her right in the eye and gave a soft growl, knowing that she would read his body language even if she couldn't hear his vocalization. He saw her tense, repressing a shiver, and his bear grumbled with pleasure. She still reacted to him physically, at least.

"I don't know how you even… God, how the hell did you find out that I work here?" she demanded.

"I know people," Luke said with a shrug.

Aubrey covered her eyes with a hand for a moment, seeming to struggle with something. Curiosity, perhaps. Anger. Hunger, if Luke was lucky. After a moment she looked at him and leaned in again, pressing the button to make herself heard.

"Look, I don't know what you're doing here. I don't know what you want, and I don't really care. You need to leave. This is…" Aubrey paused and waved a hand to indicate the shelter, "This is not the kind of place where men can show up, trying to hunt down women. It's like, the opposite of that."

Luke winced and nodded, having anticipated her reaction.

"I know. I thought it would be better to show up here than at your house."

Aubrey's mouth bunched into a displeased bow.

"Uh huh. That's not comforting. What is it that you need, exactly? Because you have exactly one minute before I call someone to escort you out," she snapped.

"I want you to go on a date with me," he said, keeping it simple.

Aubrey's mouth opened once, then closed. Her surprise was charming, and it made Luke grin.

"You…" she started, then stopped. "You tracked me

down at my place of employment, at the underground women's shelter, I might add… You did all this to ask me out?"

"Yep," Luke agreed, his grin growing broader. He was watching her body, noticing how her breaths were coming faster, how the skin on her neck and chest had begun to flush pink, how she was digging the nails of one hand into an innocent steno pad lying on the desk. She really did respond to him so beautifully, just like she would when they finally f—

"You have to leave," Aubrey said, slamming a stack of files onto her metal-topped office desk with a bang that made Luke jump. When he looked up at her, she seemed distressed and confused. Not exactly the passionate welcome he'd wanted, but…

"I'm leaving my card here, so you can get ahold of me if you want," he said, putting it on the counter.

When she banged her hand on the glass window, her frustration evident, Luke raised his hands in surrender and stepped back. He gave Aubrey one last, long look, admiring the heaving of her chest and the way she flushed under his inspection, before turning and pushing out through the security door.

Once he was back out on the street, blinking into the bright afternoon sun, Luke grinned once more.

"That coulda gone worse," he said, nodding to himself.

After all, he thought as he walked back to his rental car, at least Aubrey had reacted to him. She clearly had some kind of feelings toward him, otherwise she wouldn't get so wound up at the sight of him. He pushed down the little voice in the back of his head, the one that said that he wasn't the first man to enter the Sunnyside Women's Center looking for a woman, thinking those same kind of thoughts.

But unlike those psycho loser ex-husbands, Luke cared about Aubrey. He'd never hurt her before, and he never, ever would. He wasn't a rocket scientist, but he knew a good thing when he saw it. And Aubrey....

Damn, but Aubrey was amazing.

Whistling, he pulled his car away from the curb and headed back to his hotel. He had some more planning to do, it seemed.

FIVE

Aubrey climbed out of her VW Rabbit and stepped into the parking lot of ThanksALatte, her favorite coffee shop. Early morning light filtered through the clouds, promising another twenty four hours of gorgeous weather. Normally this was Aubrey's favorite time of day, early enough to relax in the peace and quiet, to reflect a little on herself before her busy day ahead.

Well, not today. She'd been wound up about Luke's visit all afternoon the day before, and she'd tossed and turned half the night. Now she was a cranky, exhausted hot mess. Aubrey flung open the coffee shop's front door, wincing when it banged against the wall, and stomped over to the register.

"Tall skinny chai, hot," she mumbled to the young guy working at the register.

"Aren't you Aubrey?" he asked, giving her a bright smile.

"Uh… yeah…" she said, frowning at him.

"Cool! Your drink has been paid for already. All your drinks for this week, actually. And whatever else you'd like," the kid told her.

"Is that right?" she asked, crossing her arms.

"Yeah. Some big dude came in here this morning and asked us to run it all on his card," the cashier replied.

Aubrey snorted, ignoring the guy's confused expression.

"Fine. In that case, give me ten coffees and five lattes. Along with my chai, that is," she said. "And you can expect the same order every day this week at the same time, until Luke says otherwise."

"Uh, sure. Right away," the cashier said, calling her order out to the barista.

"Great. My office is going to love this," Aubrey told him.

With that, she left a five dollar bill for tip and stalked over to wait at the other end of the counter, shaking her head.

SIX

WEDNESDAY

*A*ubrey pulled into the parking lot of her apartment building after work, still pumped up from the four coffees she'd consumed throughout the day. She hopped out of the car and tried not to skip to her front door, skidding to a stop when she spied a long white box propped against the door. It was wrapped in a velvety scarlet bow, with a card taped to the top. She leaned down and picked it up, heading inside her apartment. After dropping her keys and her purse on the kitchen table, she couldn't resist prying open the box.

Most of the box was filled with a gorgeous bouquet of blood-red roses and pure white baby's breath, all wrapped in a gauzy piece of fabric. Aubrey bit her lip, resisting any reaction. She'd never gotten flowers before, so of course she felt a little flutter of excitement. It was nothing to do with Luke, just a generally happy feeling.

Looking in the box, she fished out a DVD and a plain white piece of paper with a note on the front. The note read:

I seem to remember you saying that you liked romantic comedies. This movie comes highly recommended from my mother. Please enjoy it with my compliments, and don't be surprised when the door bell rings. You deserve a night to relax. Don't forget to put the flowers in water.

- Luke

*A*ubrey frowned at the note and looked at the DVD case.

"A League of Their Own," she read aloud. She shrugged, never having seen it.

When the door bell rang a few seconds later, she nearly jumped out of her skin. Running to the door, she pulled it open, expecting to find Luke on her door step.

"Hiya!" said a young guy holding a couple of take-away boxes.

"Uh… hi?" Aubrey said.

"Yeah, Aubrey? I got a delivery for you," he said. "You don't gotta sign or anything."

"Let me guess. A big, dark-haired guy ordered it?" she asked.

"I dunno. I just deliver it," the guy said with a shrug.

"Right. Of course. Let me just get my purse," she sighed.

"Nah, it's taken care of," the guy said, holding out the boxes to her until she accepted them. "Night, ma'am."

As she closed the door, Aubrey noticed an incredible aroma rising from the boxes. She sat them on the coffee table in the living room, opening them to find a huge, still-hot steak, steaming potatoes, a crisp green salad, and a piece of chocolate cheesecake. Before she could decide how she felt about the whole thing, her stomach gave a loud yowl of yearning, and Aubrey couldn't help but laugh.

"Alright," she said to herself. She grabbed silverware, a glass of merlot, and the DVD Luke had sent. She settled herself in, reminding herself that she could reap the benefits of his datemongering without getting sucked in.

"No problem," she murmured, taking a bite of steak as the movie began.

SEVEN

Aubrey sipped her second chai of the day, having given up on real coffee after another night of tossing and turning. Her mind wandered as she flipped through some paperwork, sighing. She needed a lot of numbers to add up this month, and as usual, she had no idea yet how she'd do it. The shelter slept ten families or up to thirty-five people at a time, and most of those arrived without a penny to their name or even enough clothes for a week. Though Sunnyside Women's Center had a large network of food pantries, clothing donation centers, and other sponsors, there was never enough to go around easily. Making the pieces fit was one of Aubrey's many jobs, and this month she was coming up a little short.

She needed to focus, obviously. Luke was a huge distraction, and she hadn't been on her game all week.

"Knock, knock!"

Aubrey looked up and smiled when she found her BFF and longtime coworker Valerie standing in the doorway, giving her an appraising glance.

"Hey, you. What's up?" Aubrey asked.

"I could ask you the same thing," Valerie said, cocking her head. "Any news you'd like to share with your best friend?"

"Uhhh… no?" Aubrey said with a shrug.

"All right. Well, you'd better come see this, then," Valerie said, turning and beckoning. Valerie led her out of the offices and through the dormitories and family rooms, into the back area of the shelter that housed the kitchen and maintenance areas.

Aubrey followed, puzzled. When Valerie led her to the small laundry room, Aubrey sighed.

"Is one of the machines leaking again? I just can't fix that this week, you know that," she told Valerie.

"Nah, that's not why we're here," Valerie said. reaching inside and flipping on the flight.

Aubrey's jaw dropped as she stepped inside. Gone were the three sets of junky, barely-working washers and dryers from the eighties. In their place were six stacked washer-and-dryer units, all gleaming a pristine white.

"Wha…" Aubrey marveled.

"Yeah. These things are so nice and new, they're even going to reduce our electric bill every month," Valerie said, giving Aubrey another appraising looks. "Now you got something you want to share?"

"No, I— Valerie, where did these come from?" Aubrey asked, throwing her hands up.

"Your new boyfriend had them delivered just a few minutes ago, and then he split."

"My new boyfriend," Aubrey echoed, confused.

"Yeah, that super hot dude that's been hanging around, asking about you…" Valerie prompted.

"Oh my god," Aubrey said, pressing a hand to her chest. "He didn't! How could he know we needed these?"

"He was asking about the shelter the other day, and I might have mentioned that we needed new machines. I was just avoiding giving out your info," Valerie said with a shrug.

"Oh my god," Aubrey repeated, turning back to the machines. "These must have cost a fortune!"

"Yeah, looks like your new man is a baller," Valerie said, her irritation growing.

"He's not my anything. He's like, trying to get me to go on a date with him," Aubrey explained.

"And you're not doing that because…?" Valerie asked.

"It's complicated. He might be kind of… stalking me," Aubrey said.

"O-kay. And you didn't feel the need to share this with me?" Valerie asked, crossing her arms and pursing her lips. She looked concerned, which made Aubrey feel a little ashamed. Luke might be coming on a little strong, but he would never actually harm her. Aubrey couldn't let Val think so poorly of the man, even if she didn't want him hanging around.

"It's just, it's nothing. He's not dangerous or anything. Just," Aubrey paused and looked around, shaking her head. "He's just weirdly determined. He's sent flowers, bought the fancy coffees I've been bringing in all week, he's showed up here trying to talk to me. That kind of thing."

"You don't exactly sound like a girl frightened for her life," Valerie said, her expression softening.

"Luke isn't like that," Aubrey said.

"Luke, huh? So why aren't you going out with Luke, the super hot guy who buys appliances for women's shelters and does nice things for you? Because...?" Valerie prompted. "Oh, right. It's complicated."

Valerie tsked and shook her head.

"Yeah," Aubrey agreed, her voice sounding weak to her own ears.

"Alright. Well, I'm done for the day and I'm off tomorrow and Saturday. Are we still on for tomorrow night?" Valerie asked.

"Yeah. Yeah, of course," Aubrey said. "I wouldn't miss it."

Valerie gave her one last look before she left Aubrey behind to contemplate the enormous gift Luke had given the shelter. After a moment, Aubrey headed back to the office and picked up her cell phone. Digging Luke's card out of her purse, she keyed the number into her phone and fired off a text.

Nice try. You can't buy me, dude. You should just give up.

Aubrey tossed her phone back on her desk with a sigh, shaking her head. This time, though, she wasn't sure if she was disappointed in Luke or in herself.

EIGHT

Aubrey sucked up the last few drops of her fruity cocktail through her straw, tilting the glass to admire the way the bar's neon lights played over the smooth surface. Up on stage, one of their co-workers was singing karaoke, a sad Patsy Cline number. Normally Aubrey loved this song, but right now she was just a little drunk and... well, okay. She was feeling a little lonesome, herself.

"Girl, you have got to snap out of it," Valerie said, leaning over and squeezing Aubrey's arm. "A guy you haven't even bothered to call didn't pay unsolicited attention to you for one whole day, and you're seriously bummed out?"

"No, no. I'm fine," Aubrey assured her friend. "Really. I think I've just had a long week, and not enough sleep. Maybe another one of these drinks will do the trick."

"Grab me one while you're at the bar, will you?" Valerie asked.

"Course," Aubrey said, slipping from her chair and heading for the bar.

Once she'd secured the drinks, she turned and wove her way back to the table just as a huge burst of laughter rose from her friends. Elbowing her way back to her empty seat, she nearly dropped the drinks on the floor in surprise.

Across from her sat Luke, dressed in dark jeans and a light gray tee that hugged his muscular physique. He grinned at something Valerie was saying, then chuckled as he accepted a high five from Nancy. Shawna leaned close to him, and Aubrey's brows shot up when she noticed Shawna actually sniffing Luke's shoulder.

"What the hell?" Aubrey asked, setting the drinks down and crossing her arms.

Everyone looked at her, but she'd already made the grave mistake of catching Luke's eye. Those stormy sea-green eyes of his seared into her, the yellow rims of his irises visibly flaring when his gaze dropped to her mouth. Aubrey shivered, though she wasn't the least bit cold.

"Aubrey, this is the guy who bought the shelter a whole new laundromat!" Nancy crowed, giving Luke's arm a playful pat. "He knows Valerie."

"Is that so?" Aubrey asked, challenging him.

"Ohh, sure. I mean, we know each other," Luke teased.

As Aubrey struggled to find the right words to shame him, the latest karaoke song ended and the DJ stood up with his microphone.

"Aaaaallllllll riiiiiiiight, ladies and gentlemen, give it up for Samantha. Wasn't she great? Alright. Next up, we have Luke! Luke, come on up here and sing for us!" the guy called.

Luke popped up off his bar stool and gave Aubrey a wink before he turned and headed for the stage.

"Uh, hey," Luke said into the microphone. "I don't usually do this, but I'd like to dedicate this song to Aubrey Rose. Aubrey, I hope this changes your mind."

The first few notes began to play, and her whole table of friends cheered enthusiastically, elbowing Aubrey and giving her encouraging looks.

"Ain't no sunshine when she's gone..." Luke sang, his face turning red as he looked out into the audience. "Ain't no sunshine when she's gooooone..."

Aubrey blinked, surprised at how nice his voice was. Luke shifted back and forth in place, looking as uncomfortable as hell, but he did the entire song without looking at the words. When he finished, most of the bar applauded wildly, some women even wolf-whistling and going up to the stage to congratulate him.

Luke headed back to the table, ignoring her suddenly-silent friends when he came around to her seat and stopped right in front of her. Aubrey's head titled back as she stared up at him, biting her lip because she didn't know what to say. Luke reached out and took one of her hands in both of his, making a warm rush of electricity spread over her skin, the hair rising on her arms.

"Aubrey," Luke said, leaning down so that his mouth was only inches from hers. Aubrey squirmed, as acutely aware of his presence as she was that of her nosy, gawping friends who were all watching with undisguised glee.

"Aubrey, will you go on a date with me?" Luke asked, giving her a private smile.

Aubrey licked her lips, letting the moment stretch before she finally nodded.

"Okay," she said.

A grin lit Luke's face at that, and he pressed a quick kiss to her wrist that had her friends oohing and ahhing.

"All right," he said. "I'll leave you to it, then."

He winked at her and then left without another word, leaving Aubrey in the middle of a whole group of excited, squawking friends. Despite their excitement, Aubrey's stomach sank. That deep, sad part of her, stuffed too far down inside to ever see the light of day, was rising. Her secret was still buried, but not nearly so deep as it should be…

NINE

"I don't know, V," Aubrey sighed, setting aside her now-cool cup of tea. She leaned back into the embrace of one of the overstuffed plush chairs in her apartment's breakfast nook, giving Valerie a considering look. Across the table, Valerie set her own cup of tea down and tsked.

"Do you have some reason not to trust this guy, Aubrey?" Valerie asked, brow furrowing. "I've never seen you so hesitant about going on a simple date."

Aubrey glanced at Valerie, unsure how to explain. Her best friend was wonderful and empathetic, but also human. No matter how close they were as friends, Aubrey could never tell Valerie about her Berserker heritage, or about the arranged mateships that the Alphas' Council were enforcing.

"I can't explain it. I just know that spending time with this guy is a big deal. Like, he's looking for something super serious," Aubrey said, shrugging. It wasn't her real reason, though it was true enough. But even Val didn't know about the aftermath of Aubrey meeting Luke the first time, and Aubrey intended for it to stay that way.

"And you're willing to deny yourself that big hunk of man just because you think he's the marrying type? You must be blind, or crazy. Or maybe both," Valerie teased, picking up her mug and taking a sip of tea.

Aubrey rolled her eyes, drumming her fingertips on the edge of the table.

"I'm fine just the way I am. I have you, I have the shelter, I have a life. I don't need more than that. I don't need a man telling me what to do, or how to live."

"Girl, what you need is to get laid! And that guy... he's got hot, steamy sex written all up and down that big, tight body of his. Go on one date, let him buy you dinner, and then take him home for a night. Wham, bam, simple satisfaction," Valerie advised, giving Aubrey a knowing look. "Or maybe you're afraid that one night will make you want more, huh?"

Aubrey couldn't help the blush that rose to her cheeks, but she shook her head.

"No. No way. I agreed to one date, and I keep my promises. So I'll go, but that will be the end of it."

The doorbell rang, and Aubrey's head snapped up.

"Expecting someone?" Valerie asked, following Aubrey as she rose and headed for the front door.

"Nope. I keep my address private, just like you do. Shelter rules."

Aubrey pulled aside the curtain next to the door, peeping outside.

"What the hell?" she murmured, opening the door. A bike messenger stood there, holding a rectangular black box tied with gold ribbon. The package was huge, three feet long and two feet wide.

"Aubrey Umbridge?" the guy asked, juggling the box as he pulled a handheld tablet from a pouch on his belt. "Can you sign for this, please?"

"Uh… okay," Aubrey said, scrawling her name on the dotted line.

"Great. Here you go," he said, thrusting the box into her arms. It was lighter than it looked, at least. At the last second, he turned back. "Oh, yeah. There's a card."

After sticking a white note card into Aubrey's fingers, he hopped on his bike and headed off.

"Special delivery?" asked Valerie, her curiosity evident.

"It seems so," Aubrey said, heading back inside and kicking the door closed behind them both. She brought the box to the breakfast nook, setting it on the table, and looked at the card.

Dinner. 7pm Tonight. The Tonga Room, 950 Mason St.
Wear one of these, if you like.
— L

"**W**ell, what does it say?" Valerie asked, practically ripping the card from Aubrey's hand. "Ooooh, L! Omigod, open the box!"

Aubrey took a deep breath and turned to the elegant black box, carefully untying the ribbon and pulling off the lid. Cream-colored tissue paper beckoned, parting under Aubrey's fingers to reveal two stunning dresses. Both were floor-length gowns, both beyond lovely. One was black, with a sweetheart neckline and delicate bronze flowers stitched from the waist down. The other was a pale pink, with a low neckline, gold seed pearls stitched at the neckline and waist, and—

"Look at the side slit in that dress!" Valerie squealed, beside herself with glee. "Ohmigod, ohmigod! Aubrey!"

Valerie launched herself on Aubrey, enfolding her in an enthusiastic hug that almost made Aubrey drop the box on the floor.

"Oops," Valerie said, pulling back. "Sorry, I'm just excited. And jealous, so so jealous."

Aubrey flipped up the hem of the first dress, turning it inside out to find the tag. Her exact size was printed there, plain as day.

"I—" she started, then paused. "Well, shit."

Aubrey sank into her chair, dropping her face into her hands. Try as she might, she couldn't stop the tears that burned in her eyes. Her bear rose instantly, ready to charge but uncertain of the target.

"Aub?" Valerie asked, instantly at her side. "What's wrong, hon?"

Aubrey shook her head, guts churning.

"He knows my dress size," she mumbled, wiping at her eyes.

"Yeah, I guess," Valerie said.

"That's so private!"

"Oh, honey. I don't think he cares about some stupid number. He's the one pursuing you, remember?"

"Yeah, because he has to!" Aubrey protested.

"What do you mean?" Valerie asked, crouching down and looking up at Aubrey.

"I can't— I can't really explain it," Aubrey hiccuped. "Luke is part of the same culture as my parents, and we're both being pressured to settle down with someone from our kind."

"Your kind? What, Anglo-Saxon?" Valerie scoffed.

"Norse, actually."

"What?" Valerie gave her a strange look.

"Scandinavian," Aubrey corrected herself. "Look, it doesn't matter. I met Luke once, years ago, and he wasn't interested in pursuing anything serious then. Now he's probably dead serious, but not for the right reasons."

"Aubrey," Valerie said, reaching out and taking her tear-dampened hand. "You're going on one date with this guy, not signing your marriage license. Pressure, no pressure, whatever. He picked a really nice restaurant, he got you two beautiful dresses, and all you have to do is just go and have dinner. It's so easy, girl."

"I don't know, Val…" Aubrey said, feeling silly.

"I'll make you a deal. If you need to bail, you text me and I'll come get you. I do think that you should go. You haven't been on a real date since—"

"Okay, okay," Aubrey said, holding up a hand to stop her friend mid-sentence. "If I call you in the middle of dinner, though, you have to come pick me up. Promise me."

"Of course I will. Now can we take these dresses into your room and start accessorizing? I'm dying here," Val asked.

"Yeah, yeah," Aubrey said, letting herself be dragged off to play dress-up.

TEN

At precisely 6:59, Aubrey stood outside the elevators on the terrace level of the Fairmont Hotel, heart in her throat. She spotted a mirror in the lobby and headed over to check her reflection one last time. She'd chosen the black and bronze dress, the more reserved of the two. With her dark red hair coiled into a loose mass at the nape of her neck, dark winged eyeliner, and ruby-red lipstick, Aubrey was starting to find her own reflection irresistible.

The mirror showed Luke's tall figure exiting the elevators, and Aubrey whirled to see him. He wore a dark, impeccably tailored suit, a pale blue shirt, and a vest of dark silk. He'd had his hair trimmed on the sides, and he'd pushed back the longer top strands in a way that suited him perfectly.

The best part was the way his eyes lit up when he noticed her approaching. His lips lifted at the corners, a dimple appearing in one cheek, and she noticed his nostrils widening. He was scenting her, even from across the room.

Her flesh prickled with goosebumps, but Aubrey held herself in check. They hadn't even greeted one another and she was already overstimulated.

"Luke," she said as she stopped before him, sticking out a hand. He raised a brow, but accepted her hand, squeezing it in his big, warm one. His thumb brushed the pulse point at her wrist, and she had to work to keep from snatching her hand back.

"You look…" He paused for a moment, his eyes traveling her figure head to toe a couple of times. "You look stunning, Aubrey. I was half afraid you wouldn't show."

Aubrey smiled and shrugged one shoulder.

"You were very persuasive," she said, turning toward the entrance to the restaurant. "Should we go in?"

"Sure. I hope you like this place," Luke said, looking a little uncomfortable. "My mother recommended it."

"I've actually never been here, but I hear it's cool," Aubrey said.

Luke reached out and took her elbow, his fingers warm against her bare skin. He guided her through the big, darkly wooded doors. The second they stepped inside, Aubrey couldn't figure out where to look. The center of the room was actually a pool, though it was empty. Dark wood booths lined the pool, complete with thatched roofs and string lights and torches. At the far end of the dining, a band played lively samba music.

"Wow! Very tiki," Aubrey said, a smile coming to her lips for the first time since she'd arrived at the Fairmont.

"It's something," Luke agreed.

He signaled to the hostess, and soon they were scooting into one of the booths. The waitress came and took their drink orders first. Aubrey ordered a hurricane, but Luke stuck to sparkling water.

"Just water, huh?" she asked, wincing when she realized how judgy she sounded.

"Uh, yeah. I really don't drink, that hasn't changed. When you saw me at the mixer, I was just trying to get through the night. It was a mistake."

"So, your mother recommended this place?" Aubrey asked, veering the conversation away from the topic of the mixer. "Is she from the area?"

"No," Luke said, shifting in his seat.

Aubrey looked at him and raised a brow. When he didn't elaborate, she decided to push him a little. It was a date, for chrissake, and they were supposed to be talking. This whole thing was his idea, and she certainly wasn't going to carry the whole conversation herself.

"Not much of a talker, are you?" she asked.

Luke turned a nice shade of red, and Aubrey almost felt bad for him.

"Tell me how your mother knew about this place," she prompted.

He cleared his throat, seeming to summon the energy to explain.

"I think she and my father did a lot of traveling when my father was in the Air Force. Once she had her third son, she made my father leave the service and settle down."

"Wow, three sons!" Aubrey exclaimed. "That's a lot."

Luke chuckled and shook his head.

"Six, actually," he explained.

"Holy shit," Aubrey said. She blushed, and her hand flew to her mouth. "Sorry. I curse a lot."

"I remember," he said, his lips twisting up again at the corners. His look said that he remembered all the other things her mouth could do, too. The heat that rose in his eyes made her cheeks go from pink to flaming red. Luke let her hang for a second longer before continuing.

"Six boys, yeah. Ma says that's why they picked Montana to settle down in. Lots of room for us to ramble."

"Montana… Wait, was the Lodge your place?" Aubrey was dumbfounded.

"Yeah, that's my family home. We're the Beran clan," Luke said. His tone held a note of pride, something Aubrey had never felt about her own clan. They were very traditional and not especially feminist-friendly, so Aubrey didn't waste much time on feeling any particular way about them. Luke, it seemed, had a different kind of bond with his clan.

"The Lodge is beautiful. I think I actually talked to your mother for a while, she was explaining the history of the area," Aubrey said. She took a sip of her drink and picked up the menu.

"Ma is really interested in history. Native American history, specifically. She thinks it parallels a lot of Berserker history. Being driven away from our lands, being some mythological thing that's overblown, half of it invented for white men to tell stories…" Luke waved a hand, shaking his head. "I'm not explaining it right. You'll have to talk to her about it."

Aubrey raised a brow at the presumption in his words. Luke just gave her that half-smile again, but didn't walk back his words.

"Maybe," Aubrey said, shaking her head. She buried her face in the menu, only to feel a soft tug moments later when Luke pulled it from her hands.

"There's a family-style thing," he said, spreading her menu wide and turning the page. "It's got a little of everything. Will you share it with me?"

"Egg rolls, pork ribs, sichuan beans, roasted suckling pig…" Aubrey read aloud. "That's a lot of food, Luke."

For a horrifying second, she wondered if Luke thought she required some huge pile of food at each meal.

"You've seen me eat before, Aubrey. I run ten miles

a day, five or six days a week. Plus I'm a bear. I need a lot of calories just to survive," he teased.

When Luke gave her a sweet, genuine smile, though, she melted a little. He hadn't lost an ounce of charm since San Diego, that was certain.

"I don't seem to remember you getting out of bed to go running," she said, surprised at her own flirtatious tone.

"I may be crazy, but I'm not dumb enough to leave your bed, Aubrey. Besides, I think we got plenty of exercise together, don't you?"

Aubrey flushed again, dropping her gaze from his. Still, she couldn't help but smile. Their two-day-long sex-a-thon really had been impressive.

"So, the family dinner?" Luke prompted.

"Sure," she said. As she agreed, her stomach rumbled in anticipation, and Aubrey was glad she hadn't insisted on a salad as she usually did on first dates. Then again, this wasn't exactly a first date, was it?

"Alright," Luke said, waving the waitress down and ordering for them both.

"It'll take about thirty minutes, if that's alright?" the waitress asked.

"Sure, sure. Can you bring her another one of those drinks?" Luke asked. The waitress nodded and rushed off to put in their order.

They sat in silence for half a minute, Luke looking Aubrey up and down like some kind of prize he desperately wanted to win. And then, in a flash, he changed.

A man at the table behind them shoved out of his booth with a shout, losing his balance and knocking several glasses off the table. The second the glasses shattered, Luke's entire body tensed. His expression turned dark and guarded, his mouth forming a cruel line. He shot to his feet and whirled on the drunk man, chest heaving, and nearly upset their own table in the process. If Luke had been in bear form, his teeth would be bared and his fur standing on end. A warning of something dangerous to come.

"Luke!" Aubrey said. When he didn't respond, she stood and reached out to him, giving his arm the lightest brush with her fingertips. "Hey. Luke, hey. Look at me, okay?"

Luke turned his attention away from the now-trembling drunk man. His gaze came to rest on Aubrey, and she was surprised to see how dark his eyes had grown. She'd seen it before. Many times, actually. Her father was a Vietnam veteran, and he had the same reaction every time a car backfired.

"Hey," Aubrey said again. "It's just you and me, okay?"

Luke swallowed hard, letting his shoulders drop a little.

"Okay. Sorry. I, uh…" He sucked in a deep breath and sat down, looking embarrassed.

"No, don't worry. There's no need to apologize," she

said, picking up her napkin and sitting down again. Twisting the napkin in her fingers, she tried to think of the right way to ask him about his history.

"So you were in the Army, right?" she said.

"Yeah," he agreed. The distraction seemed to be working, because he was slowly growing more relaxed, focusing on her words. "Almost a whole decade, you know?"

"I bet you've already staked out every door in this room, huh? You have an exit strategy already?" she asked.

Luke's lips curved up, and he gave her a slow nod.

"Through the back left door. It empties into a hallway that leads out to the Terrace," he said.

"You checked this place out already?" she asked.

"I got here before you, actually. I used the restroom in that hallway, and then went back down to the first floor in case you were there."

"Ah! I must have been on the other elevator, coming up to meet you, then. Passing like strangers in the night," she teased, fluttering her eyelashes and giving him her most charming grin. Aubrey felt pleased that Luke looked more relaxed, seeming more chatty than before.

"How'd you know about the exit strategy thing?" Luke asked, his eyes intent upon hers.

"My father was in the service. Army, like you. He fought in Vietnam."

"Does he jump at every little noise, too?" Luke asked. Aubrey couldn't miss the self-scorn in his tone.

"Not at all. My mom says that when Dad got back, it just took him a little while to get comfortable again. There's only a couple of things that set him off now, and I think that's mostly habit. He's a stubborn son of a bitch," she said.

"The Army seems to turn those out in large numbers," Luke said. He hesitated for a moment. "I really am sorry about that, a minute ago. I guess I'm trying to get comfortable again, too."

"Don't be sorry. I've heard it helps if you can identify the sounds and smells that trigger you. Is glass breaking one of them for you?"

Luke dropped his gaze to the table, staring at his folded hands.

"Ahhh… Glass breaking, anything even remotely loud and low, airplanes, helicopters, men shouting. Actually, anybody shouting. Electronic beeps, like pagers. They sound like what you hear a few seconds before an IED goes off."

He glanced up, sheepish.

"I could go on," he admitted. "It sounds crazy, I know. It's already getting better, though. My first week back was a lot worse."

"How long have you been back?" Aubrey asked, curious.

"Just a month."

"That's a long furlough," she said.

"No, um, actually. I'm retired from service," Luke said.

"Oh! I had no idea. I mean, how would I have known, I guess." Aubrey felt flustered all the sudden. "Sorry. I have the weirdest feeling right now, like we know each other, like we've known each other for years, but that isn't really true, is it? We're kind of… just meeting."

Luke nodded.

"I know just what you mean. I feel like I know you so well, though. Maybe that's just because I spent so much time thinking about you when I was doing my tours."

"About me?" Aubrey asked, surprised.

"Well, yeah. I mean, it's really lonely over there, so all the guys spend a lot of time thinking about women. But I also wondered about you a lot. Where you were, what you were doing. Why you left without giving me your number. You know, that kind of thing."

"Ah," Aubrey said, biting her lip.

"Plus, I needed some good memories. That weekend we spent together… I've never had anything else like it."

"Me either. I wish…" she trailed off.

"You wish what?" Luke asked

"I wish I'd been in a better place when it happened. I was so happy that weekend, and that's all you got to see. But I wasn't happy in my life back then. I'd just come out of a bad situation, and I needed to be on my own."

"So you took off?" Luke challenged her, though he kept his tone soft.

Aubrey shrugged, feeling foolish.

"Yeah. I was freaked out, and hurting, and you… you're such a keeper. You deserved someone who wasn't all fucked up, you know?"

Luke reached out and covered her hand with his, his lips pressing into a frown.

"I should have tried harder to find you, Aubrey. I thought about it all the time."

Surprise fluttered in Aubrey's chest.

"You did?"

"Yeah, of course. Look at you. You're fucking incredible. How could I not think about you?"

Before Aubrey could reply, several waiters arrived with steaming platters of food. They heaped the table with sizzling cast iron dishes, leaving an astonishing array of choices before Aubrey's amazed eyes.

"Man, this looks incredible!" Luke said, his excitement clear. Aubrey almost laughed at his quicksilver change from intense and emotional to hungry and jubilant.

"Alright, let's dig in then," she said. Passing him a plate, she did as she commanded.

ubrey threw back her head and laughed as Luke spun her on the dance floor. After the Tonga Room, Luke had whisked her a few blocks away to a jazz club. Though she didn't know much about that kind of dancing, the dark dance floor was packed with swaying couples as lights flashed and music pulsed under her feet. Aubrey wasn't one to dismiss new opportunities, so she'd let Luke lead her out onto the dance floor.

Luke took the lead from the first step, pulling Aubrey into his arms and right up against his body. Aubrey couldn't help her reaction; her bear rumbled to life, curious about Luke's proximity. Her body didn't miss his closeness, either. She could feel a full-body flush sweep her from head to toe as Luke's warmth and strength seeped into every inch he touched.

Though he was clearly experienced on the dance

floor, he kept things slow and led Aubrey step by step until she started to feel more comfortable. Soon she was letting her feet do all the work, just relaxing and people watching as she enjoyed being in Luke's arms.

After they'd warmed up a little, Aubrey pulled the pins from her hair and let it tumble free. There was nothing quite like seeing Luke's gaze heat when he'd caught a lock of her hair, exploring the silky length with his fingertips. He didn't say anything, but she remembered how much he'd loved her thick, dark hair during their weekend together. The way he kept brushing his fingers over it, leaning close and sucking in lungfuls of her scent, made her certain that he still felt the same.

"Are you having some deep thoughts down there?" Luke teased her. He looked down, giving her that same soft smile, the lift of his lips as his eyes sparkled. It really was killing her slowly, Aubrey decided.

"No. Just thinking that this is comfortable," she said with a shrug. The song ended, sliding into another. Aubrey looked up at Luke as he led her into the next number, thinking how nice it was that she could trust him to take charge. Aubrey was always in charge of everything in her life, and just this once it was nice to be able to step back and let go.

"What's comfortable?" Luke asked, making easy conversation.

"Just, you know. I thought it might be awkward, since we were both kind of nervous at dinner. And I don't really know how to dance. But it's not. We're kind of…" Aubrey trailed off, trying to think of the right word.

"Good together?"

Aubrey chuckled.

"Maybe. I don't know if I would go that far. I was thinking earlier that it's hard for me to find dates sometimes. Not because of my size, I mean—"

Luke's brows shot up, and he interrupted her thought.

"I should hope to hell not!" he snorted.

Aubrey rolled her eyes and shook her head.

"Plenty of guys are interested in bigger girls, although some of them are creeps. Like fetishists and stuff," she said, pursing her lips.

"I'm so glad you didn't lack for dates with other men," Luke said, his tone going dry.

"Listen, I was trying to pay you a compliment before you interrupted me," Aubrey scolded.

"Oh, by all means, then," Luke said with a smile.

Aubrey huffed, but Luke's hand on her waist drew her a hair closer and she couldn't bring herself to pull away.

"I was trying to say that I have trouble finding dates because I'm the picky one. I only want to date guys who are sort of big and brawny, guys who make me feel dainty," she admitted, pulling a face at herself.

"First of all, you are perfectly dainty. Second of all,

those other guys just aren't Berserker males, so they just pale in comparison."

Aubrey laughed at his temerity.

"Is that right? You bears are all just big, godly men meant to be worshiped?" she asked.

"Hey, hey. I'm just talking looks and size here. And I think you might remember a little bit about that, huh?" Luke asked, his eyes darkening as he gazed down at her. Luke pulled her flush against his body, pressing the long, thick length of his erection against her through their clothes, as if there was any way she'd forgotten.

Aubrey's mouth dropped open, but for the life of her she couldn't come up with a decent response to that. Her cheeks burned, too, because he was more right than he knew. Aubrey remembered exactly how impressive his cock was, and all the ways he'd used it to make her cry out his name, over and over.

"Wow, I can't believe I just managed to get the better of you," Luke said.

"Yeah, well. Don't get used to it, buddy," Aubrey said.

"Mmmhm. Well, you know what I could get used to?" Luke asked.

"I'm afraid to ask," Aubrey said, her breath hitching as her body brushed against Luke's again.

Luke stopped moving in the middle of the dance floor, one hand at her waist and the other coming up to cradle her head. He watched her intently, his eyes like emerald fire, warning her of his desire and giving her time to flee.

Aubrey let him tilt her head back, let her breasts crush against the firmness of his chest as he leaned down. Her eyelids fluttered closed of their own volition when she felt the heat of his breath fan over her lips, her tongue darting out to dampen them. Her heart thudded in her chest, the music pulsed all around them, and Luke's body against hers seemed to still time.

The first brush of his lips was a tease, a question. Luke was asking for permission, something he'd never done back in San Francisco. Aubrey couldn't have pulled away if she'd wanted to; her body and her bear yearned for Luke, and her heart was too full of sweet, hopeful butterflies.

So she went up on her tiptoes, bringing her mouth against Luke's warm, firm lips, relishing the shudder that went through his body. That was encouragement enough for Luke, whose grip tightened on her body, fingers threading into her hair as his tongue traced the seam of her lips. They hung in the moment, suspended in a warm, safe bubble, as Aubrey's lips parted under Luke's explorations.

The moment that the tip of Aubrey's tongue touched Luke's, a spark caught between them. Suddenly Luke's hands were everywhere at once, roaming her body just as hers did his. Her arms went around his neck, pulling him closer. Their lips and tongues danced and darted, moving in rhythm with each other and the music. Aubrey's teeth caught and tugged Luke's bottom lip, eliciting a deep growl of desire from him. She could feel the vibration from his chest, making her shiver. Making her bear rise to the surface, just as she knew Luke's did.

They both sucked in breaths between kisses and nibbles, and Aubrey gave a long, loud moan when the heat of Luke's mouth found a sensitive spot on her neck. In the back of her mind, she knew that people had to be watching them, but she couldn't bring herself to care. One of Luke's hands cupped her breast for a tantalizing moment before slipping down between them to press against her mound.

"Yes," Aubrey breathed, knowing that Luke could hear her over the music. She melted against him, her need growing like an uncontrollable flame, threatening to burn her alive. She needed him naked, muscles straining, crying out as she rode his cock. She needed him to bend her over, spread her knees, and fuck her until she didn't know her own name.

She needed—

Luke's teeth scraped her neck, testing, and Aubrey pressed upward on her tiptoes. She needed everything that Luke could give her, every hot, pleasurable second of it, and she wanted it now, public be damned. Her bear knew what she needed, and she needed the bite.

Luke's teeth brushed that spot again, the exact spot where Berserkers marked their mates, and something new and dark and hungry pulsed within Aubrey's body.

A need she'd never known before burned there, a desire that couldn't be reined in. When Luke stiffened and paused, his mouth leaving her neck, Aubrey cried out and pounded her fist against his shoulder, unable to control her want.

"Aubrey, wait," Luke said, his big hands coming up to shackle her wrists.

Aubrey's eyes opened, and she stared up at him for an endless moment, balancing on the edge. She grappled with her desire, with her bear, as she slowly became aware of the situation.

"Shit!" Aubrey said, shaking off his touch and stepping back.

"Aubrey, I'm so sorry. I let things get out of control. I didn't know it would be like that," Luke said. Aubrey looked at him, really looked at him. His pupils were huge, his body trembling, and he sucked in ragged breaths. She'd provoked him, pushed him too far, and now he was hanging by a thread. And yet he'd still been the one to pull back, to stop them both from doing something foolish.

"It's fine," she said at last shaking her head.

"No, it's just... I don't want to rush you," Luke said, reaching out for her hand. Aubrey avoided his touch shaking her head.

"No, I mean... there's nothing to rush here. We're just... you know, horny or whatever," she said, growing flustered.

"Aubrey, it's more than that. For me, at least."

"Look, can we just go? It's late, and I've probably had too much to drink," Aubrey lied.

Luke's eyes widened at the last, and Aubrey instantly felt bad for making him think that he'd taken advantage of her.

"I didn't realize," he uttered, shame blooming in his expression. "Of course we can go."

In a matter of moments they were out on the darkened street, the fresh air creating a space between them like nothing else could have. Luke hailed a cab, his expression angry, but somehow Aubrey knew it wasn't directed at her. Luke was nothing if not honorable, and he honestly thought he'd wronged her. It made her feel like a complete bitch, but she didn't know how to take back her words.

A big yellow cab pulled up, and Aubrey climbed inside, trying to think of the right thing to say to him. To her surprise, Luke went around the other side and climbed in next to her.

"Uh… I can cab it by myself," Aubrey said, confused.

"I'm not leaving you by yourself," Luke scoffed.

"Really, I'm not even that tipsy. I'll be fine," Aubrey promised.

"Not happening," Luke told her. He turned his attention to the driver and gave Aubrey's address from memory, surprising her yet again.

The cab ride was quick and quiet, depositing them outside Aubrey's apartment building in record time. Too soon for Aubrey's lust-addled brain to have processed things and come up with something good to say. When Luke got out and ushered her out of the car, Aubrey expected him to wish her goodnight and be on his way.

Instead, he surprised her again by flat-out refusing her offer of cash for the fare and dismissing the cab.

"I can get into my house just fine," she promised him.

Luke shot her a quelling look as he paid the cab driver, and Aubrey couldn't help the goosebumps that broke out over her bare flesh as he followed her right up to the door of her apartment. His brooding expression was hard to interpret, some mix of self-condemnation and sense of duty and straight-up lust, if Aubrey had to guess.

"We need to talk, Aubrey. Invite me inside," Luke commanded.

Aubrey took a second to soak in the masculine glory of him. He was so tall and muscular, with that gorgeous dark hair and those sexy blue-green eyes that hid just a hint of yellow at the center. Dressed in that tailored suit, he was a walking fantasy, and one she couldn't pretend she didn't want.

But fantasy or no fantasy, this was all happening for the wrong reasons. If Luke wouldn't shut down this mating farce, Aubrey certainly would.

"We can talk right here," Aubrey said, lifting her chin in an intentional gesture of defiance. Luke's gaze narrowed, but he didn't argue with her. He was far too much of a gentleman, and of course he had his own pride besides that.

"I didn't mean to move things too fast earlier," Luke said. His frankness shouldn't surprise her, Aubrey knew; he'd never been anything but forthright and open with her. Still, cutting right to the heart of an issue wasn't easy, and she liked the honesty of it. She resolved to try to tell him how she really felt in turn.

"I could invite you in," Aubrey said, wrapping her arms around herself and heaving a sigh. "I could pour us some wine, and we could chat for a minute, and then we could get naked, which I think is what we would both like right now. I could do that."

Luke's lips twitched, and she could tell he was picturing the scene just as she was. Aubrey steeled herself and continued, trying to cut out all the bullshit and save them both some trouble.

"But I'm not the two-night-stand type of girl, not like I was in San Francisco," she explained.

Luke looked startled for a moment.

"I never thought of you like that, I swear," he said.

"Well, there's only two reasons for us to be standing here right now," Aubrey said. "One, for a quick hookup. Two, to fall in line with this crazy mateship thing that the Alphas' Council cooked up. And Luke, no matter how handsome and smart and funny you are, I'm not here for either of those. I like my life, I like the way things are. I'm not looking for some knight in shining armor to come rescue me, just like I'm not looking for meaningless sex."

"And I don't want that from you," Luke said, his dark brows drawing down into a scowl.

Aubrey let out a groan of frustration.

"Look. You've made it clear that you… desire me. You tracked me down and hounded me for a date. You're fulfilling your duty, just like all the other children of Alpha bears. I get that, believe me."

"Are you saying that you only accepted my invitation because you're fulfilling your duty?" Luke snapped. Aubrey could read the hurt in his expression, and though she regretted putting it there, she knew she had to push forward until he understood.

"Luke, I had a nice time. But I'm just not interested in being a tic on some checklist. I'm not taking a mate, and I'm not taking you to bed. Go find some other girl to meet your quota, okay?" Aubrey shot back, folding her arms.

Luke stared her down for several long seconds before shaking his head in disbelief.

"Honestly, Aubrey. I can't decide whether your ego is massive or non-existent. You're a complete mystery to me."

"Yeah, well. Go figure someone else out. We're done here," Aubrey hissed. Though it killed her bear, she turned her back on him to unlock her apartment door and let herself inside. When she slammed it closed, she checked the peephole and caught his retreating figure as he stormed off through the parking lot.

Aubrey locked all three of her deadbolts, and gave a deep sigh.

"Excellent people skills, Ms. Umbridge," she whispered to herself. She looked up at the clock on the foyer wall and realized that it was only 10:30, so she had a little time before she needed to head to bed. She needed a distraction.

"And for your reward… a glass of wine," she said aloud.

Aubrey changed into a pair of soft flannel pajama pants and a soft white camisole, then poured herself a big glass of merlot and a big glass of ice water. She parked herself on the couch and leaned her head back, groaning as she replayed the night's events. Her bear was anxious and lonely, her body still wound tight from Luke's touch.

Had she just made a huge mistake?

Closing her eyes, Aubrey decided that she couldn't worry about that now, because there was no different outcome to be had. Luke was amazing, but there were things she just couldn't tell him. She'd agreed to one date to placate him, and she'd done that. Now she needed to get back to living her own life. After just a few sips of her wine, she let herself drift off.

TWELVE

When Luke heard Aubrey's footsteps approaching, he gave a sigh of relief. He stayed put, sitting on her doormat and waiting for her to appear. He wanted to get up and move around, shake some sensation into his legs, but he didn't want to startle her unduly. She didn't see him right away, and he had almost a full moment to simply admire her from afar.

Aubrey wore a simple knee-length black dress and a white cardigan. Her long hair was twined in an elegant braid that wrapped all the way around her head, making Luke's fingers itch to unwind it so he could run his fingers through the soft strands. Her eyes were downcast as she walked, her expression solemn, but that didn't take away from her beauty in the least.

When she was only a dozen feet away, she finally saw him and stopped dead in her tracks.

"Jesus H.—!" Aubrey screeched, nearly dropping the brown paper grocery bags she held in her arms.

Luke winced and raised a hand, giving her an awkward wave.

"Sorry. Hey," he said.

"What the hell are you doing here?" Aubrey asked, giving him a scowl. Not the expression of pleasure he'd hoped for, honestly.

"Waiting for you," he said with a shrug.

"Waiting for how long?" she asked.

"Uh…" Luke checked his watch. "Three hours."

Aubrey stared at him for a long moment and then heaved a sigh.

"You'd better come in, I guess," she said, maneuvering around him to unlock the door. Quick as a flash, Luke was on his feet and taking the grocery bags from her, trying not to get underfoot as she led him into her house.

"Your place is nice," Luke said, glancing around at her apartment. Everything was done in light wood and pastels, giving the apartment a beachy feeling. It wasn't what he would have imagined for Aubrey, but it was clean and bright and soothing.

"Thanks," Aubrey said, her voice flat.

Luke followed her, setting the groceries down on the kitchen counter. He watched her move around the kitchen and put everything away, waiting patiently for her to finish. When she was done, she turned to him with an expectant expression.

"Let's sit," he said, gesturing to the living room. He headed to the couch without waiting to see if she'd follow; somehow, he knew that she would. Aubrey didn't like taking orders, but she was too curious to walk away. He took a seat on the couch and waited.

"Alright. You're here, you've got my attention," Aubrey said, canting her head to one side as she perched on the opposite end of the couch. Her hands came to rest in the middle of her lap, bunching up the thin cotton of her black dress. He could tell that she was more anxious than she let on, could smell it on her. A note of lust lay under that, as well, but Luke ignored that for the moment.

"You know I don't… talk a whole lot," Luke began. Aubrey's eyebrows raised, as if to say no kidding. "I've always been kind of reserved, even with my family. My brothers used to tease me, say that there was nothing going on inside my head. Nothing to talk about, you know?"

"I've never thought that," Aubrey said, looking surprised.

"Yeah, it's stupid. Just an old joke. But it's true that I like to listen, and that I don't share much with anyone else. Especially after some of the stuff I saw in the Army, it's kind of hard to relate to most people. They're talking about baseball, and my head is all full of…" Luke paused, making a circle in the air next to his head as he contemplated the right phrasing. "War, I guess. I don't know how to make small talk, never have.

Between being a Berserker and being military, I don't have anything in common with anyone. It's easier to listen to them talk about their hobbies and opinions than to tell stories about some of the stuff I've seen."

"It's okay, Luke. You don't have to explain," Aubrey said, scooting a little closer and putting her hand on his knee. The gesture warmed him, but he knew he had to focus. He needed to finish explaining things to her, tell her how he felt for once instead of just holding it all inside.

"When you talk to me, I listen because I'm interested. You do your work at the shelter, which I think is awesome. You talked about your family a little, and I can definitely relate to that. You talk about people you know, and why their stories are interesting, and I can tell that you like to listen, too."

Aubrey looked thoughtful, but she just nodded. Proving his point.

"I've known your name and your city since the day you left San Diego," he said, switching tactics.

"You— Wait, you have?" she asked, looking shocked.

"Yeah. I got it from the front desk. I knew who you were and where you were, and I planned to come find you the second my feet hit American soil again," he admitted.

"But that was years ago," Aubrey rebutted.

"I know. I'm telling you that part because I don't want you to think that I only came to find you after I saw you at that party at the Lodge. I don't want you to think that I only came here because of some fucking decree by the Alphas' Council, either. So I want to tell you why I didn't come find you sooner."

Luke turned his hand over, catching Aubrey's fingers and lacing them with his own. She didn't respond, but she did give him a soft, encouraging smile.

"I can't tell you a lot of the specifics, but some really bad shit happened right after I left San Diego," Luke began. "There was a lot of killing, really up close and personal. And it wasn't just the enemy attacking us, either. I did a lot of things that I regret, even though it was my job and I was following orders. Even though not doing those things would probably have gotten me killed, I still feel like hell about it."

Aubrey squeezed his fingers, tears glinting in her eyes as she listened to his story. Luke's gut churned, wondering if telling her all this would drive her away. If she had any idea what he'd actually done, the way he'd killed so many. The idea turned his blood to ice, made him sick inside.

Luke's mind transported him back to the camp in Jordan. He heard the shooter's footsteps, saw the glint of a weapon. He'd dropped to the floor before he was even aware of his own movements, breath catching in his throat as the kid's boots snicked across the sandy wood floor of the bunk room. He pictured the surprised faces of his team as they turned to face their death. Then the gun was in Luke's hand, the bullet flying away from him, and the kid's brains were everywhere. A perfect head shot, something the team referred to as "a Beran Special". His special, special move—

"Luke! Luke, hey!" Aubrey was saying, tugging at his hand.

Luke looked down at her, torment raging in his chest, and understood something.

"No wonder you can't love me. I'm a fucking killer," he said, rising from the couch. He needed to leave Aubrey's house. Drive off into the sunset and never return.

"SIT. DOWN."

Luke froze. He turned back to Aubrey, finding her seething with anger. He could barely believe that commanding voice had come out of his petite Aubrey. Her chest heaved, her fists were clenched, and her expression was enough to chill him.

"I said, sit the fuck down. You are not leaving this house right now," Aubrey ordered. She sat down, staring at him in challenge until he mirrored her movement. He wasn't much for taking shit from anybody now that he was out of the Army, but the look on Aubrey's face said that she wasn't afraid to shift and try to fight him. If they threw down, Aubrey might get hurt, and that was unacceptable.

"Are you done talking now?" Aubrey asked. Luke could see that she was keeping a tight rein on her bear, even as he struggled to do the same.

"Yeah," he said.

"Good. I want to hear your story. Not right now, but soon. I want to hear the whole thing, because it's clear you need to tell it," she said.

"Half of it is classified, Aubrey," Luke snapped.

"I don't give a shit. If you're here, supposedly courting me as your mate, I deserve to hear it all. And not because I'm disgusted, or think you're a bad person, but because that's what mates do."

"Aubrey—"

"No arguments. I can't be angry that you didn't come chase after me, especially after the way I left, but I sure as hell can be mad if you can't use these newfound talking skills of yours to tell me your whole story."

Luke hesitated, his stomach still leaden, but after a minute he nodded his acquiescence.

"Fine. If that's what you really want, Aubrey. But if it's show and tell time, I want to know why you were so sad when I first met you. Why you had the most incredible weekend of your life with me, and then you just walked out on me without a word. There's a story there, too."

Aubrey sucked in a deep breath, her eyes widening.

"Do I need to repeat all the things you just threw at me?" Luke asked.

Anger flitted over her face for an instant, chased away with resignation.

"Fine. Fair's fair. You tell me about your lowest

moment, and I'll tell you about why I was standing in that bar in San Diego, trying not to cry."

Luke's heart squeezed at the way she dropped her eyes, showing him her shame.

"Hey," he said, reaching out and tipping her chin up. "We don't have to talk about that any more tonight. All right?"

"Right," Aubrey said, letting out a breath. "Not tonight."

Luke pulled her into his arms, inhaling deeply of her unique scent and relishing the soft warmth of her body against his own. Somehow, holding her close like this, trying to chase away her pain with an innocent touch, was almost harder than admitting to the woman he loved that he was a killer.

Luke looked down at her, his gaze dropping to her lips. Before he knew what he was doing, his mouth was on hers. This time, her lips parted under his right away, giving him access. He sucked in a breath at the sweet, distinctive taste of her lips, a honeyed delight quickly branded into his senses. He cradled her jaw in one big hand, sweeping the other down her shoulder to grip the plushness of her hip.

When Aubrey leaned forward to press her body closer to his, Luke's animal side took over. He grabbed her hips and picked her up, settling her onto his lap. The soft chuff of surprise that escaped her turned him on like no other. He felt his body hardening, muscles tensing as his cock came to full attention.

The soft weight of her on his lap made him want to groan out loud. He sought her mouth again, his tongue teasing and tasting as he ran his hand down to explore the bounty of her ass. She was so soft and warm under his touch, as if she were made for his pleasure.

Aubrey pulled back for a second, uncertainty plain on her face.

"Luke, I'm not sure we should do this," she said, sounding a little breathless. He wanted to reassure her just as badly as he wanted to take her, so he settled on a compromise.

"I'm going to stay clothed," he said. "Let me make you feel good, no strings attached."

"Luke… are you sure?" Aubrey asked. The excitement in her voice, the hunger in her eyes… it was going to be the death of him.

Luke pushed her back onto the couch, giving her a slow, deep kiss before peeling off her cardigan and dress. Underneath she wore a black lace bra and a sexy pair of red panties that made his cock twitch with want as he knelt before her. Just as she had the first time he'd undressed her, she blushed and tried to cover herself. Luke was having none of that, catching her hands and pushing them up behind her head.

"Don't move these," he said, giving her hands a squeeze before releasing them.

Aubrey bit her lip and nodded, her eyes gone dark with desire. Luke put a hand on each of her knees, skating his touch up the top of her thighs. He felt

Aubrey shiver as she watched him, anticipation making the fine muscles in her thighs flutter and tighten. Luke grabbed her hips, parting her legs as he pulled her to the edge of the couch. The scent of her desire flooded his senses as he brought her heated core right up to press against his own body. He surged forward just once, rubbing his erection against her to remind her of his size and all the amazing things he could do to her.

Aubrey gasped and writhed. She moved her hands, but a deep growl from Luke had them back in place instantly. Luke might be lost in everyday civilian life, but the bedroom and the battlefield were his element, the two places where his Alpha was truly free. He wasn't about to let Aubrey forget it, either.

Lifting his hands to her shoulders, Luke slid the black satin straps of her bra off her shoulders. He brushed butterfly kisses over the tops of her breasts as he edged her bra cups down and down until finally she was bare to him.

"God, your tits…" he marveled, lifting them in his hands. They were more than bountiful, each far more than he could hold in one hand. Perfectly round, pale orbs tipped with lush, velvety nipples. He leaned in and nuzzled the curve of one breast, dropping kisses and nips of his teeth as he worked his way inward to one pebbled nipple.

Aubrey cried out and sank her fingers into his hair as he closed his mouth over her sensitive flesh. He rolled his tongue over and around it, teasing the tip with his tongue and teeth until she was panting and bucking her hips against his cock, driving him wild. He gave her a soft nip, making her back arch with surprise and pleasure. Squeezing her breast in his hand, he switched his attentions to the other one. Licking, teasing, scraping his teeth over the most sensitive part, he was rewarded with her plea for more.

"Luke, please!" Aubrey breathed. He drew back and licked his lips, loving how her eyes followed the movement of his tongue.

"Please what?" he asked, weighing her breasts in his hands, brushing his thumbs over her nipples.

"I need…" she began. Before she could finish, Luke hooked his fingertips in the top of her panties and tugged them down. Aubrey released a breath and lifted her body, helping him strip her naked. Luke glanced up at Aubrey and noticed that she was blushing, despite how turned on she was.

"Look at you," he growled. "You make me so fucking hot, Aubrey. Your body is so perfect. I can't wait to taste you."

He moved back and leaned down, spreading her thighs wide. Her bare, pink slit glistened with her excitement, and Luke couldn't resist sampling her. He parted her lips with two fingers, using the tip of his tongue to trace a hot line from her core up to her clit. Aubrey tensed under him, sucking in a breath. Luke closed his lips over the tender bud, sucking and swirling his tongue over her most sensitive spot until she cried out.

"Luke, Luke…" Aubrey moaned.

Luke slid a single thick finger into her hot, tight core and nearly came himself when her inner walls tightened around him. He withdrew and slid in two fingers, licking and sucking her clit as he thrust his fingers into her channel over and over. When he felt her tense once more, her orgasm growing close, he added a third finger and fucked her relentlessly, sucking up every bit of her sweet juices as he brought her to the edge.

Aubrey hovered on the brink, her cries growing desperate. Luke repositioned himself as he worked, using his free hand to explore. He sent one juice-slicked fingertip past her tight, full core and up until he circled the tight circle of her ass. He flicked and fluttered his tongue over her clit as he circled his fingertip around the rim, invading her sensitive flesh with the barest fingertip.

Aubrey screamed as her orgasm took her in a sudden jolt, making her muscles lock up as she bucked her hips against Luke's mouth and fingers. He kept sucking and pumping his fingers until she moaned and pulled his head away. Only then did he rise, wiping his lips as he returned to sit next to her. Luke pulled Aubrey's limp form into his arms, reclining on the couch as she struggled to catch her breath.

As he held her, he kissed the top of her head,

inhaling her scent and feeling her heart beating wildly against his chest. After she'd calmed, they lay together for a long time without speaking or moving. At last, Luke knew he had to leave. He didn't want to rush Aubrey into anything, or demand that she change her life for him. Not yet, not until she knew that was her own heart's desire. He couldn't stay the night tonight, and he needed to tell Aubrey about his plans for the rest of the week.

"Aubrey, I'm going to leave in a minute," Luke said.

"You don't have to go," she said, but he could feel her body tense against his. She was ready to shield herself, ready for him to push her too far.

"I do, actually. I have to get some things in line. I have a job interview in Portland on Friday, so I'll need to head back Thursday night. Just to be on the safe side," he told her. "Always a boy scout. I like to be prepared."

Aubrey snorted, but he could tell by her expression that his announcement was irritating her.

"Alright. So… that's that, huh?" she asked. Her tone was casual, but her body was even more tense than before.

"Uh, no. I have to leave for a couple of days, but I'm coming right back. And I'm not even leaving for three days. I'd like to see you again tomorrow or Wednesday, if possible." He'd gone through the schedule in his head a dozen times, trying to figure out how much he could see her before his plane took off.

Aubrey was silent. As usual, not the boundless enthusiasm he wanted from her, but at least she hadn't kicked him out of the house yet. At least she was being still, letting Luke hold her in his arms.

"You're job hunting in Portland," she said at last. A statement, not a question.

"Yeah. This has been on the books for weeks. It's a great position, actually. Something I might actually like and be good at."

Aubrey gave him an odd look that he couldn't decipher, and then squared her shoulders.

"I need to ask you something," she said. The expression on her face nearly made him wince, because he could tell that she was going into battle mode.

"Okay, shoot," he said, taking a deep, calming breath.

"The decree from the Alphas' Council that we should all take mates… How much did that factor into your decision to come find me?" she asked.

Her tone was harsh, as though she already found him lacking and didn't want to hear his excuses. Luke blinked, feeling a little shell-shocked even though her question was not unreasonable or even unexpected.

"Well… In some ways, a lot. In some ways, none," he replied.

Aubrey crossed her arms, her mouth tightening into a scowl.

"Right. Gotcha," she said.

"To be honest, I always assumed you had a mate. I

was planning to track you down anyway, out of curiosity, but I wasn't in a rush about it. When my parents announced the mateship thing, you popped into my head. Then I saw you at the mixer, and knew you were still available…" he said.

Luke cleared his throat and shifted in his seat, feeling uncomfortable explaining his motives and thought process. He wasn't even getting it half right, either. He'd obsessed about her, thought about finding her, been elated when he'd known she hadn't taken a mate.

"Okay. Well, thanks for being honest," she said.

Aubrey pulled out of his gasp and grabbed her dress, tugging it on over her head and covering herself. Luke stood, knowing that he was being thrown out on his ass.

"Can I see you before I go on my trip?" Luke asked.

"I'm not—" Aubrey paused, blowing out a frustrated huff. "Let me think about it."

"Okay. If not, just let me know. I can wait until I get back, I just don't want to," he said.

Aubrey gave him another of those odd, undecipherable looks.

"Goodnight, Luke," she sighed.

Luke leaned in and dropped one last kiss on her lips, and then headed out.

"Lock the door behind me, okay?" he asked.

Aubrey shot him a glare, but followed him.

"Bye—" he said on her doormat, only to have the door shut in his face.

As he walked away, he gave a low whistle.

"Well, shit," he told himself. "That did not end well."

Luke kept moving to his car, refusing to give in and run back to her door for the second time. A man had his pride, after all. Shaking his head and cursing the serious case of blue balls Aubrey'd given him, he headed back to his hotel.

THIRTEEN

*A*ubrey swirled the last sip of her cocktail in its glass, gazing at all the gorgeous people packing Wilson & Wilson, her favorite fancy bar. Though Aubrey knew that Val just wanted the latest gossip about her situation with Luke, when Val had invited Aubrey out for drinks, she couldn't resist. A champagne cocktail and some girl talk had sounded like just the ticket to her mateship blues.

So they'd dressed up and come downtown right after work, early enough to score a good table at the popular bar. Three drinks later, Val was pushing Aubrey for details on her date with Luke.

"That's it? You guys hooked up, but didn't go all the way, and then you kicked him out?" Val said, disbelieving. "You should have hit that, girl. He's sooooo hot."

"Yeah, he really, really is," Aubrey sighed. "But I told you, I can't figure out his motives."

"Luke seems like a pretty decent guy to me," Val said with a shrug.

"They all do, at first. And with Luke… I can't really explain it, but I think he's just interested in me because his family wants him to settle down, and he thinks I'd sort of… fit the bill. Not very romantic." Aubrey pulled a face.

"Yeah, but couldn't he basically just date whoever? From everything you've told me, he's kind of a catch."

"I told you, we're from the same culture," Aubrey said.

"Oh, yeah. The Norse thing," Val said, rolling her eyes. "That's a pretty lame connection, if you ask me."

"It's really important to our families."

"But not to you, it seems," Val noted.

"No, not to me. My father promised me years ago that I wouldn't have to deal with any of this shit."

"Was that…" Val hesitated. "Does that have something to do with all that vacation time you took a few years ago?"

Aubrey's gaze snapped up to her friend's face. She'd taken three months off from work, claiming that she was going abroad to refresh herself. In reality, she just hadn't been able to face her day-to-day life after her engagement with Lawrence had gone off the tracks. She and Valerie hadn't been as close back then, so it surprised Aubrey that Val had figured out that her 'vacation' had been tied into the demands of her crazy family.

"Ah. Um, yeah," Aubrey said, unwilling to get into the whole tale.

"I figured your absence was guy-related. You and that guy Lance were getting pretty serious—"

"Lawrence," Aubrey corrected automatically. Even as the words left her mouth, she wondered why she even cared.

"Yeah. Well, you guys were all hot and heavy, then you told me you might break it off, and then…" Valerie shrugged. "You were gone. When you came back to work, you never talked about it, but you stopped going on dates. Luke must be your first date in… I don't even know how long."

Aubrey nodded, knowing that her friend was right. She had waited way too long between men. Now her lust was uncontrollable around Luke, making it hard for her to think clearly when he was around. Not an ideal situation when her future freedom and happiness might be at stake.

"Hey. Earth to Aubrey," Val said, waving a hand in front of Aubrey's face. "I didn't mean to send you down some kind of rabbit hole, buddy. I was just curious."

"I don't want to talk about the past anymore. Should we have one last drink before we hit the road?" Aubrey asked.

Val shook her head.

"I can't. One more drink would mean leaving my car here for the night. Between the valet and the Uber rides, it would bankrupt me," she joked. Val's figure was slimmer than Aubrey's, something Aubrey occasionally coveted. Still, Val's petite frame meant that she couldn't hold her liquor worth a damn.

"Alright. Let's get moving, then," Aubrey said, signaling the waitress to bring the check.

After Aubrey and Val hugged and parted ways, heading to parking spots in opposite directions, Aubrey's phone rang. Fishing it out of her purse, she was surprised to see that it was her parents' home number. It was almost nine at night, way later than her mother felt it polite to make phone calls.

"Hello?" she answered.

"Yeah, uh, hey," came her father's gruff voice.

"Dad? Hey, is everyone okay?" Aubrey asked, her stomach fluttering with sudden nerves.

"Yeah. Uh, yeah. I just… I got word that a Berserker stopped by the clan compound, looking for information about you. I was calling to make sure it wasn't anything…" Her father paused, seeming uncertain. It was an unfamiliar sensation, as her father was an Alpha and a bully, right down to the marrow in his bones. He hadn't even called to check in after the Lawrence fiasco, preferring to let Aubrey's mother handle what he called 'her hysterics'.

"I'm not in any danger," Aubrey told him, rolling her eyes with gusto. "It's just someone I knew a while ago."

"Who is he?" her father demanded.

"Luke Beran, if you must know."

There was a moment of perfect silence on her father's end.

"Beran. So you're following the decree, then? Finding yourself a mate?" he asked.

"I agreed to go to the mixer, and I did. There's nothing more going on."

"Luke Beran is from a good family. He'd be a good choice," her father told her.

"You made me a promise, Dad. You promised that you'd never put me in the same situation again, never pressure me to settle down with a mate," Aubrey chided him.

"So you know this bear, but you don't want him as a mate?" her father clarified.

"Correct."

"Fine, fine. Be stubborn," her father sighed. "Your mother wants you out at the house tomorrow. We're grilling with some of your aunts and uncles and cousins."

Aubrey could see it now, all her relatives swarming and chatting and scarfing down Uncle Reid's famous ribs.

"Is Mom making her mac and cheese?" Aubrey wheedled.

"Course she is."

"Alright," Aubrey acquiesced. "What time?"

"We eat at one. Come a little early and visit with your mother. She misses you."

No mention of her father's own feelings about his only child, of course.

"Fine," she ground out.

"Fine," her father said, and the line went dead.

Aubrey stared at the phone in her hand, shaking her head. What the hell had she just agreed to?

FOURTEEN

"Uncle Reid really does make the best barbecue on the planet, hands down," Aubrey said, wiping her lips with her napkin before pushing her plate away.

"I wish I could eat like, five more plates," her cousin Emmie agreed.

They sat together at one of several picnic tables laid out in Aubrey's parents' back yard, a large patio area complete with a pool, outdoor kitchen, and even a wet bar. Her parents loved to grill out, and they did it in style. Fifty or more Berserkers were here for the party, nearly half of Aubrey's clan. The broad expanse of the back yard was enclosed by a thick tree line, making the event feel safe and private. It was an ideal meeting place, since a lot of the group would probably shift and explore the forest later.

"I think one more plate would kill me," Aubrey said

as she watched the bear shifters mingling. So far the gathering had been pretty sedate, not a single fight breaking out. Then again, the guests had been here for less than an hour. Not enough time or booze to get anyone riled up… yet.

There had been a tense moment when Aunt Lilah had pointed a finger in Aubrey's father's face and shrieked, "Jack Umbridge, you son of a bitch!" Moments later, Lilah giggled and launched herself into her brother's arms, and the whole party relaxed and went back to the business of chowing down.

"Killed by ribs?" Emmie snorted. "We're all being sent into forced mateships anyway. Maybe death by barbecue isn't such a bad demise."

Aubrey laughed, casting a discriminating eye over her favorite relative. Emmie and Aubrey were definitely swimming in the same gene pool, looking so like one another that as kids, their own parents had sometimes confused them. Nowadays, where Aubrey tinted her hair to bring out her natural reddish highlights, Emmie's short chestnut locks were natural and curly.

"What?" Emmie asked, sipping her Corona.

"I was just thinking that about how you and I used to be mistaken for one another as kids," Aubrey said.

"Yeah. I mean, Sarabeth looks like us too," Emmie said, pointing to another cousin who stood across the yard, socializing. "And Ann, and Becky. Wow, I just noticed that there are only two kinds of women in our family. Big, dark-haired, and busty, and thin, blond, and brainless."

Aubrey giggled, knowing that they were both looking at their cousins Jenna and Leslie. Both women did fit the 'thin, blond, and brainless' ticket.

"What about Samantha?" Aubrey asked, nodding in the direction of yet another cousin. "She's thin and blond, but she has a PhD in spatial physics. She's basically a genius."

"Ugh," Emmie said, shaking her head. "She's super nice, too. Way to ruin things for the rest of us."

They both cracked up, relaxing as they sipped and people-watched. It was a welcome distraction from the rest of Aubrey's life.

"Whoa…" Emmie said, setting her beer down and grabbing Aubrey's arm. "Please, please tell me that's not a cousin."

Aubrey followed Emmie's gaze to see that Luke had just emerged onto the patio, Aubrey's father on his heels. Half the women on the patio turned to scope Luke out, admiring him in his light blue plaid button-up and well-fitted dark wash jeans.

"Oh, god. Is he here with one of the blond cousins?" Emmie moaned.

"I doubt that," Aubrey said, but Emmie wasn't listening.

Luke smiled and nodded at Aubrey's father, that beautiful oceanic gaze of his roving the back yard until he landed on her. Aubrey shivered, feeling strangely exposed. How the hell was Luke here at her family home, meeting all her relatives?

Luke broke away from Aubrey's father, making a beeline for Aubrey.

"Omigod, he's coming over here!" Emmie gasped.

"Yep," Aubrey said. "Of course he is. He's here to see me."

"What?" Emmie asked, but there was no time to explain.

"Hey," Luke said. Aubrey looked up from her seat, her eyes soaking up every tall, lean inch of him as he towered over her.

"Hey," she said, confused. "What are you doing here?"

Puzzlement lit Luke's features, but Aubrey's father pushed his way into the conversation before anything became clear.

"Uh, Luke. Got some people I need you to meet," her father said, reaching out and ushering Luke away from Aubrey's table.

"Jack—" Luke started. Aubrey's dad cut him off, steering him directly into a group of the 'thin, blond, brainless' types who were gathered around another table, all staring Luke down like he was the last rack of Uncle Reid's ribs.

"You know him??" Emmie asked, swatting Aubrey's arm. Aubrey swallowed and nodded, but she had no words to explain things.

Aubrey's father handed Luke a cold beer and

ordered him to sit down at the table. After another glance at Aubrey, Luke complied. One of the blondes gave a dazzling smile, laughing as she touched Luke's arm.

Jack Umbridge made a beeline back to Aubrey, raising a brow. He crossed his arms and stared down at Aubrey, a satisfied look on his face.

"See? I fixed it," her father grunted.

"Fixed what?" Aubrey asked, crossing her arms.

"I meant what I told you. You don't have to take anybody you don't want. I said you had my protection, so…" He waved a hand at Luke. "I'm giving Beran something else to occupy him. Problem solved."

Aubrey opened her mouth, preparing to blast her father for butting in, but he held up a finger.

"Hold that thought. Looks like Beran's getting bored," he said.

Luke stood up, giving one of the cousins a forced-looking smile, and tried to brush off another cousin's touch. The way Jenna, Leslie, and Mary were fussing over him made Aubrey realize that not everyone was fighting against the forced-mateship decree. Her cousins seemed ready to go all in, right here and now.

"Shit," Aubrey muttered. She stood up, looking around for her mother. Locating her in the far corner, Aubrey skirted her father and Luke and all the cousins.

"Mom, what the hell?" Aubrey asked, frustrated.

"Is there a problem, Aubrey?" her mother asked, raising a brow and crossing her arms.

"Why is Dad doing this? I didn't ask for help getting rid of Luke." Without meaning to, Aubrey found herself mirroring her mother's agitated pose.

"You gave him quite the guilt trip, missy. Your father isn't a talker, he's a doer. So he went out and did," her mother said.

"But—"

"Hey," her mother said, shaking her head. "I don't want to hear it. For all you know, this guy—"

"Luke. His name is Luke," Aubrey snapped.

"Okay. For all you know, Luke might make a connection with one of your cousins."

"He most certainly will not!" Aubrey protested.

"Do you have a claim on him?" her mother challenged.

"No! No, nothing like that." Aubrey scowled at her mother.

"You don't want him. That's what you're telling me," her mother stated.

Aubrey took a deep breath, heat rising in her cheeks. She nodded, unwilling to back down.

"All right then. Go get yourself a fresh beer and go back to Emmie. She looks lonely. Even better, make an introduction," her mother suggested.

Across the yard, Aubrey watched as her father introduced Luke to a gaggle of dark-haired women. Leslie followed them, inserting herself into the new group as she turned on her charm full-throttle. Luke looked over at Aubrey for a brief moment before turning his back, focusing his attention on one of the pretty brunette cousins.

"This is ridiculous," Aubrey muttered, shaking her head in disgust. She left her mother's side, scooping up two fresh beers as she returned to Emmie's table.

"Is there something going here?" Emmie asked as Aubrey sat back down.

"Nope. Nothing worth knowing," Aubrey said.

They clinked their beer bottles together and sipped, sitting back to watch the show.

FIFTEEN

When James Erikson, current Alpha of Aubrey's pack, showed up with a small entourage, Aubrey really started to feel nervous. Erikson brought his mate and a flock of young, eligible women from his own family. Aubrey waved to Therese, James's daughter. The beautiful, curvy brunette was sweet, smart, and vivacious; her girl-next-door personality mixed with her good looks made her the quintessential "It" girl. Aubrey hadn't seen Therese since the night of the Beran family's social mixer, but her presence here could only mean one thing.

Apparently Luke was a hotter commodity than Aubrey realized. Aside from being a catch, as Val mentioned, he was in a position of power. As the oldest son of Josiah Beran, he had the potential to run the affairs of every Berserker in the Pacific Northwest.

With his military background, he was no doubt a strong contender in the eyes of every Alpha.

That thought made Aubrey realize that she'd never bothered to ask Luke if he planned to succeed his father. The idea of it put her off; Aubrey hated the idea of being a doting socialite, something inherent in the role of an Alpha's mate.

"This is getting serious," Emmie said, nodding to James as she returned to the picnic table. With Aubrey's nod of encouragement, even sweet Emmie had presented herself to Luke, curious about his presence.

"Any luck with Luke?" Aubrey asked, keeping her voice neutral. Jealousy was burning her up inside by now, but she had no right to say anything.

"Really?" Emmie sighed, drumming her fingernails on the table.

"What?" Aubrey asked, tearing her gaze from where James was introducing Luke to Therese.

"Quit pretending like you don't care. I saw the way he looked at you when he arrived, all intense. And you can't stop staring, so…" Emmie waved a hand.

"I'm just interested in what's going on. Everyone else is watching," Aubrey pointed out. It was true; every single person in the backyard was monitoring Luke's interaction with James and Aubrey's father with great interest.

"Oh, here he comes!" Emmie squeaked.

Luke was heading straight for their table, anger

clear in his expression. Everyone still watched him, several of the women looking put out.

"Would you excuse us?" he asked Emmie. She scurried off to stand with her mother, leaving Aubrey alone with Luke. Though they were several yards away from everyone else, Aubrey felt the heavy weight of her clan members' scrutiny.

"Aubrey, what's going on here?" Luke asked her, crossing his arms and leaning against the table. Aubrey cleared her throat and pushed away the empty bottle she'd been toying with.

"It seems like you're being courted," Aubrey said, pressing her lips into a hard line.

"If this is your idea—" Luke began, stopping short when Aubrey's father stepped up and put a hand on his shoulder. James Erikson was right behind him, looking foreboding.

"We've got two offers on the table," Jack Umbridge said, acting as if Aubrey was invisible. "My niece Leslie is… taken with you."

"Or my Therese," James cut in. James and Aubrey's father stood shoulder to shoulder across from Luke, leaving Aubrey staring up at them like a child. "Either one would be a fine choice. It would bring our clans closer together."

Aubrey's jaw dropped. The sheer political manipulation happening here was astounding. She looked at Luke, who was looking more and more irritated by the moment.

"I just need a second to talk to Aubrey," he said. "Alone."

"No," her father said, his tone and expression going flat. "Leslie, or Therese."

The hot blond or the stunning brunette? Aubrey wondered, feeling bitter.

Luke tried to move to see Aubrey's face, but the two Alphas shifted to block her entirely.

"I can't decide something like this within a few minutes," Luke said, his frustration evident. "I didn't even know that this was a matchmaking event."

"You'll go out with one of them, then?" James demanded to know.

There was a long silence, every second of it making Aubrey's guts churn. She pushed up from the table, not wanting to hear any more. Turning, she fled toward the front driveway. She needed to get in her car and get the hell out of here before this got any more claustrophobic.

"Don't you dare move," she heard her father's booming voice following her.

Tears burned at her eyes, but she refused to look back. A tiny voice inside her head told her to turn around, tell Luke that she was interested, that she cared for him… But if she couldn't commit to a mateship, that would be wrong. Aubrey jumped in her car and fled, knowing that she was sealing her fate, and probably Luke's in the bargain.

Luke leaned against the side of his rental sedan, watching the front door of Sunnyside Women's Health Center. He tapped his foot impatiently, glad at least that he was out in the open air again.

He'd come straight here after his flight back from Portland; all the noises and strangers and standing in line had nearly killed him. To top it off, his obvious agitation had once again drawn attention from airport security, resulting in a long, overly thorough, clenched-jaw search and questioning. His bear was so close to the surface now, roaring to be released. Nothing good would have come from that.

His phone buzzed in his pocket and he checked it, finding a message from Aubrey's friend Valerie.

Good to go. She's on her way out, it read.

Luke cleared his throat and pushed off the car when

the front door swung open. Aubrey appeared, dressed in a stunning light blue dress and red heels. Her long hair was twisted into a thick braid that lay on one shoulder, and Luke couldn't remember her every looking more beautiful.

She juggled a huge stack of files in one arm with a tote bag and a purse, looking down as she walked toward him. It wasn't until she was almost even with his car that she looked up, stumbling and nearly dropping her paperwork.

"Luke, what—" Aubrey cut herself off, shaking her head. "Shouldn't you be off honeymooning with one of my cousins by now?"

Luke frowned at her, shaking his head. He wasn't about to let her pick a fight here on the street.

"Get in the car," he ordered, leaning over to open the back seat. "Give me your stuff, I'll load it up for you."

"I'm sorry?" she asked. He loved the look of surprise on her face, just the moment before she geared up to rip him to shreds.

"Get in," he repeated.

"I don't think so," she snapped, turning to leave. She ran smack into Valerie, who'd walked up behind her carrying a small duffel bag. At Valerie's expectant expression, Aubrey scowled.

"You two are in cahoots?!" Aubrey cried, stamping her foot. 'This is ridiculous! You are such a traitor."

Valerie crossed her arms and raised a brow, giving Aubrey a hard stare.

"I'll remember that you said that," Valerie replied.

"So, what? What is this?" Aubrey asked, flustered.

"Get in the car, and I'll tell you," Luke said.

Aubrey shoved her files into Valerie's arms, turning to confront Luke. She was nothing short of a spitfire, and Luke had to admit he liked seeing her like this. More than liked it, actually. He could sense her bear rising, bringing his own to the surface, and in his too-long-celibate state, it excited him on a primal level.

Before she could open her mouth to protest any further, Luke stepped forward and grabbed her by the waist. Pulling her close, he did what he'd been longing to do every second since she'd kicked him out of her house: he kissed her. He leaned down and planted his lips firmly against hers, holding her tightly. For a long moment she resisted, her body tensing as if she would push him away.

Then her mouth softened under his, her arms coming up to his shoulders. Her lips parted on a sigh, and her tongue sought his. In seconds the kiss was deep and feral, leaving them both panting. Aubrey moaned against his lips, and it was everything Luke could do not to strip her down and take her right there on the sidewalk. His bear finally relaxed a bit, letting Luke breathe easily for the first time in days.

Though he wanted nothing less than to release Aubrey from his arms, Luke slowed the kiss and then pulled back, looking down into her desire-darkened eyes.

"Get in the car, Aubrey," he said softly. "We're going on a trip."

"I can't," she breathed. "I have work, and I don't have anything packed."

"That's where I come in," Val interrupted, waving a hand to remind Aubrey that she was still present. "I went to your house at lunch and packed you a bag. And I've got your work covered for a few days, however long you need."

Aubrey stepped back, looking up at Luke with an expression that was mixed with fear and longing.

"What is this about?" she asked again.

"I guess you'll just have to get in the car to find out," he shrugged, playing it cool.

After an agonizing minute, Aubrey sighed and accepted the duffel bag that Valerie held out to her. Luke grinned as he tucked her in the passenger seat, stowing her bag in the back. His heart felt light, though he knew that this was only the first step. The hardest part was yet to come.

ubrey was quiet for most of the hour-long trip up the coast. Luke drummed his fingertips on the steering wheel and changed the station half a dozen times, feeling fidgety. The city was wearing on him, making him jumpy despite Aubrey's calming presence. His time in Portland hadn't treated him too well; he'd regressed and nearly had a full-blown panic attack at the airport.

Aubrey just smiled at him every time he attempted small talk, so he shut up. She unbraided her long hair and combed it out with her fingers, filling the car with her warm scent. Luke shifted in his seat every few minutes, embarrassed that her scent was making him hard as a rock.

When Luke pulled off the highway and turned into a lightly-forested private drive, she watched out the window but didn't say anything. He stopped the car at the end of the road, a quiet spot where the tree line broke a few hundred yards from the ocean.

"This is us," Luke told her, hopping out of the car. He opened the trunk and pulled out a tent, two coolers, and a duffel bag to match Aubrey's. He was bouncing on his feet, the tension inside him expanding, building up restless energy until he thought he might explode.

"Is that a tent?" she asked, eyeing him with suspicion.

"Sure is. Not to worry," he told her, producing a thick foam pad from the trunk. "It's going to be plenty comfortable."

"I don't really camp out," Aubrey said, looking down at her heels in dismay.

"Ah, yeah. Valerie packed you some shoes," Luke said, handing over her bag. Aubrey opened it, pulling out a pair of pink flip flops. She frowned and plucked at a piece of red satin inside the bag. Her eyes lit with recognition after a second, but she just blushed and muttered something nasty about her friend as she zipped the bag closed. She left her heels in the car, slipping into the sandals.

Once she was ready, Luke led her over to their destination. Their home for the night was a broad wooden platform with four tall corner posts. It sat just under the first line of trees, overlooking the white sand beach.

"Okay. There are drinks in the blue cooler, there," Luke gestured. "Just sit back and watch me work."

Aubrey obeyed for once, and in minutes Luke had a thick tarp strung up from the posts. He assembled the tent just as quickly, putting the foam pad down inside. He went back to the car for an armful of soft pillows, which he tucked inside the tent.

"What do you think?" he asked, waving to the tent.

"Very nice," Aubrey admitting, a smile playing on her lips.

"Not done yet!" Luke told her. He made short work of gathering a huge stack of firewood, setting everything up for the campfire he planned after dark. He settled all the bags and coolers in their places, refusing Aubrey's offer of assistance. Once he was done, he frowned and rolled his neck, trying to release some of the tightness in his shoulders and back. He'd thought that getting out of the city would quiet his bear and ease his own nerves, but it hadn't helped a bit.

"Hey," Aubrey called, sitting on the platform next to the tent. "Come sit with me for a second."

Luke glanced at her, admiring the way her long hair fluttered in the fresh salt air, the early evening sun making the strands gleam like silken fire. He trudged over and settled down next to her.

"What's going on with you?" she asked, giving him a piercing look.

"Nothing," he replied, his words the same automatic defense he used with everyone in his life.

"Bullshit," she said, shaking her head. "You're so…

tense. You've been wound up since the second I laid eyes on you."

Luke blew out a breath. He wasn't ready to lay his baggage on Aubrey's shoulders.

"It's just been a long week, that's all," he said. It sounded lame, even to his own ears.

"You need to shift," Aubrey told him.

"It's… I can wait," he edged.

Aubrey scooted off the platform, kicking her flip flops off into the sand. She turned and walked into the trees, glancing back at him plaintively. When her dress hit the ground a few feet away, Luke couldn't help but follow her. He stripped and changed into his bear form, hearing the familiar creaks and snaps of bone as she shifted just out of sight.

Aubrey padded back to him in her bear form. He stilled as he saw her, spotting the tawny splash of fur at her chest that stood out from the rest of her thick, dark pelt. She was a sun bear, something he hadn't expected. Aubrey was much smaller than his own Grizzly form; in this shape, she was probably only two-thirds of his size. His bear adored her immediately, recognizing her without a hitch.

Aubrey gave a soft snort, turning and heading off into the woods, leaving him to trail behind. Luke followed, realizing that both his human and bear sides were completely lost on Aubrey Umbridge.

EIGHTEEN

*L*uke finished packing away the remains of their dinner, packing them away in the car.

He returned to Aubrey, groaning as he sat down next to her on the tent platform. With a soft wool blanket spread out beneath them and the fire crackling just a few feet away, sitting and watching the last rays of sunlight fade was a comfortable exercise.

"Sore?" Aubrey asked, her voice teasing.

"Yeah. I haven't really run in my bear form since I was at my parents' house," he admitted.

"It's hard to get a good run when you live in the city," Aubrey said, her voice wistful. "I have to go out to my clan's land. It kind of sucks making time in my schedule."

Luke nodded, though he didn't have much of a schedule to worry about just yet. Once he took a job in the city and settled into a routine, things would get harder.

"The trip to Portland was pretty rough. I should have called James Erikson and asked permission to run on his land before I went. I just didn't want to end up on a surprise date with his daughter," Luke joked.

"It's hard to say no to Therese," Aubrey said, twisting her fingers together in his lap.

"Not for me, it isn't. She's very nice, but she's not you."

Aubrey looked up at him, her brow creasing, but she didn't directly respond. Instead, she skirted the topic.

"You met plenty of women at my father's party."

"And what an event that was. When your father called me, I thought— Well, I'm not sure what I thought. I hoped he was trying to put us in a room together. It didn't take long for me to see that I was totally wrong about that," Luke said with a chuckle.

"I was wondering how you ended up there," Aubrey said, pursing her lips.

"Yeah. Your father is pretty persuasive when he wants to be."

"No kidding," Aubrey said. "He's the reason I went to that stupid social mixer in the first place. No offense to your family or anything, but that kind of forced interaction isn't for me."

Luke laughed. He took a deep breath, realizing how much better he felt after a run and some fire-grilled salmon and vegetables. Like any bear, his life grew exponentially harder whenever he was the least bit hungry.

"My mother does love to throw barn parties, but the speed dating aspect of it wasn't her choice. My dad volunteered her services."

"Hah! My mom would freak. My dad might be the Alpha, but the house is my mom's domain. She runs the show there."

"My mother never argues with my father in front of anyone, even me and my brothers, but she does run our lives. She's the one who got me the interview in Portland, actually. The company is owned by a friend of the clan, someone who happens to work in the tech side of security."

"That's what you do?" Aubrey asked. Luke nodded.

"I do the hardware stuff, all the gadgets."

"That's what you did in the Army, then?"

"Yep. Ten whole years of my life," Luke said.

"So… Portland, huh? When you take the job, you'll be pretty far away from San Francisco."

Luke chuckled.

"I like that you assume that I got the job."

"Well you did, didn't you?" Aubrey said. It was nice that she seemed so certain of him.

"I mean, maybe. If I did, it's because of my family connections. I bombed the interview, hard."

Aubrey looked up at him, wide-eyed.

"How?" she asked, as if such a thing was impossible.

"I had a panic attack about five minutes before I went in. It was so much pressure, and I was thinking about things with you, and I smelled smoke..." He sighed. "Turned out, someone just had a door propped open and there was a food truck parked outside. But I really lost it."

"I'm sure it wasn't that bad," Aubrey said, reaching out to put her hand over his.

Luke gave her a half smile.

"You weren't there. It wasn't good."

He hesitated, unsure whether he should share his coping technique.

"What?" Aubrey asked, watching him closely.

"It's going to sound stupid, but I use our time in San Diego to kill my panic attacks," he said.

"Really?" she asked, looking amused.

"Yeah. I think about lying in bed, eating room service steaks with you."

"And you drank that sparkling apple juice instead of champagne," Aubrey giggled, reminiscing.

"Yep. If anything, my whiskey experience at my mother's barn party reinforced that I am a firm non-drinker," he said.

Aubrey went silent at his mention of the mixer, a dozen negative emotions flitting over her face.

"Can I ask you something?" Luke said.

"Sure," Aubrey shrugged, her light mood gone.

"After you left your parents' house the other day, your dad cornered me and lectured me. He was belligerent. He wouldn't be straight with me, exactly, but he did say something to me. He said, 'because of Lawrence', something about some guy named Lawrence."

When Aubrey flinched, Luke instantly regretted his words. Surely she would withdraw now, refuse to talk any more. Instead she looked right up at him, eyes glimmering with the beginning of tears.

"I guess I do have some explaining to do," she said, her voice breaking. When Luke opened his mouth to silence her, tell her she didn't have to explain a thing to him, she shook her head.

Luke could do nothing but sit back and wait for her story to unfold.

NINETEEN

*A*ubrey took a deep breath, dropping her gaze from Luke's face. It was time for her to get the story out in the open, to let him make of it what he would.

"Lawrence is Lawrence Matheison," she started, pausing.

"Like the Matheison clan in Chicago?" Luke asked. Aubrey blinked, giving a slow nod. Luke was far too clever.

"The same. He's Anders Matheison's only son, the heir to the Alpha title."

Luke nodded but didn't say anything else. He did reach out and take her hand, wrapping her fingers in the warm strength of his own. Aubrey rubbed her fingers against his, savoring the soft callouses. Luke was strong, and he worked with his hands when he could. He was salt of the earth, nothing at all like Lawrence.

"He's really good looking," Aubrey admitted, nearly smiling at the way Luke tensed and bristled at her words. "Settle down. I'm just saying that it's part of his charm. He lets everyone know that he can get any girl in the world, and when he looked my way… I'm ashamed to admit, it swayed me. I was young and easily impressed."

She took another breath before continuing.

"He kind of swept me off my feet. Flowers, candy, fancy dates. He took me out on his father's yacht, all the time telling me how lucky I was, how I was a special girl. I wanted to hear that so badly. Growing up around all my gorgeous cousins, who you've met…" Aubrey flapped her hand.

Luke shrugged, noncommittal.

"Well, he bowled me over. It's funny, because he didn't actually give me any of the things I wanted in a relationship. He got down on one knee on the fifth date, promised me a huge ring, all that. But he wouldn't live with me first. He wouldn't attend any gatherings with my family, only his. He always talked about how he was going to move me to Chicago, and he wouldn't hear of anything else."

"And you let that happen?" Luke asked, looking amused. "I can't imagine that."

"I had reservations, but everyone else was so thrilled. My parents were over the moon, and the

Matheisons were so nice to me. Lawrence brought me to Chicago for a week and dumped me on his mom half the time, pushing us to plan this huge wedding. It wasn't what I wanted, but everyone kept telling me that the two clans being joined through marriage was this important social event. It made me feel important, and I got caught up in it."

She stopped for a moment, remembering.

"In retrospect, Lawrence slipped a few times back then. He'd laugh at my suggestions, call them stupid. I brushed it off. He was a terrible flirt, always talking to other women, but when I got mad he'd just flatter me until I let it drop. The big red flag was that he barely ever touched me, no matter how romantic the dates were. He said he was waiting until marriage."

Aubrey gave a disgusted snort.

"Such a lie, but I didn't think anything of it. I actually think his mother tried to warn me away a few times. She kept asking me uncomfortable questions, but she was totally cowed by Lawrence and her mate. I actually saw Lawrence grab her and twist her arm once, but she acted like it was no big deal… that's when I knew things weren't working out."

"So you broke it off," Luke guessed.

"Well, I confronted him about his behavior, and he lost it. Totally dropped his sweet fiance act, called me nasty names. He told me that if I messed things up for him, he'd make me regret it. This was like… four days before the wedding."

Luke's jaw tensed, his hands clenching.

"He sounds like a piece of trash."

"Yeah, well. He was all apologies the next day, but I knew I had to tell my parents what was going on. When they got to Chicago, I sat them both down and told them some of what I'd seen. My dad went ballistic, almost as bad as Lawrence, telling me to shut up and fly straight. My mom was sympathetic, but she assured me that I was just getting cold feet."

"That's… I don't know what to say about that," Luke said, his eyes flashing with his growing anger.

"They don't either, now," Aubrey assured him. "Honestly, the whole thing might have gone forward, regardless of my wishes. It just snowballed until I couldn't do anything to slow it down."

"I hope you left that asshole at the altar," Luke grumbled.

"We didn't get quite that far. Lawrence disappeared from the rehearsal dinner, this fancy-schmancy affair. When I got up to go look for him, I found him In one of the back rooms of the banquet hall, balls-deep in one of the bridesmaids he'd picked out for me. A child-hood friend, supposedly."

"I'm guessing he was repentant?" Luke asked.

"Not in the least. Actually he flew off the handle. Called me fat and worthless, told me that I'd better get used to him doing as he pleased, because no mate of his could tie him down. He told me that I was nothing, that I was just a way for him to rule over two clans, some crazy bullshit like that. He grabbed me and started hurting me, just like he did with his mom. I tried to fight back, but I was just so stunned. I didn't even think to shift," Aubrey said, her embarrassment acute. "It's the lowest I've ever felt in my life. My dad showed up a few seconds later, and he had to pull Lawrence off me."

"And your father didn't kill him on the spot?" Luke ground out.

Aubrey looked up at him. His eyes were blazing now, the yellow in his irises standing out starkly. His fury was so strong that Aubrey could actually scent it in the air, swirling around them, almost chokingly thick. She reached out and stroked her hand down his arm, relieved when her touch seemed to take the edge off his volatile mood.

"Honestly, I think we were both just so ashamed. My dad felt like shit for forcing the whole thing on me, and not listening when I told him what was going on. And me… I was just destroyed. It sounds stupid, but I felt like it was all my fault. Like if I'd been better, Lawrence would have wanted me for me."

"Jesus," Luke said, seeming floored.

Aubrey hesitated, realizing that this was the moment. She'd told him half the story, and he'd barely batted an eyelash. If she told him everything, it might drive him away, but at least she would feel honest. She owed him the truth.

"It wasn't all bad. I actually met Valerie through a support group for victims of abuse. She brought me to

Sunnyside to volunteer, and we both ended up working there. It changed my life, but not all for the worse," she said.

Taking a deep breath, she laced her fingers with Luke's and looked up into his eyes.

"That was only a few months before I met you," she told him. "And… there's more to the story, honestly."

Luke's mouth opened and then closed again. Aubrey couldn't help but smile, because though he was the quiet type, she'd actually never seen him speechless before. Even as she smiled, tears welled in her eyes as the words formed on her lips.

"I thought about finding you, too," she confessed. "In fact, I was planning on it. I had even met with a private investigator who might have been able to track you down."

"But you didn't," Luke said, tilting his head to the side, watching her closely.

"No. A few weeks after we spent the weekend together, I missed my period." Aubrey sucked in a deep breath and released it, knowing that there was no turning back now, she needed to get the whole thing out. "I went to the doctor, and she confirmed the pregnancy."

Luke's eyebrows shot up, his surprise coupled with a tinge of suspicion.

"I wasn't in the right place in my life to have a child. I was still reeling from things with Lawrence, and then I got pregnant with a virtual stranger…"

"We weren't strangers. Not after the first night we spent together," Luke said, his voice gone to gravel.

"Just let me… I need to tell you everything. I knew I couldn't have a child. I knew my parents would force me to keep it, that I would be chained to them, or to you if I ever found you. I just… I just couldn't do it. So I made an appointment to terminate the pregnancy."

Aubrey exhaled, long and slow.

"I don't want to hear any more, Aubrey. This is… I don't know," Luke said. The hurt in his expression broke her heart, but she needed him to understand.

"I never went to the appointment," she said, shaking her head. "After all that, I still couldn't do it. I changed my mind, decided that I'd have the baby and give it up for adoption."

"Are you trying to tell me that I have a kid out there somewhere, living with strangers?" Luke said, his voice rising dangerously.

"No. No, I'm afraid not. I miscarried in the third month," Aubrey said, her voice shaking. Tears broke free, rolling down her face, and she closed her eyes.

"You…" Luke started, then stopped. He stood up, brushing himself off, and rubbed a hand through his hair. "I just… I need to take a walk, think for a minute. Please don't go anywhere."

The look on his face froze Aubrey to her spot. She nodded, a whimper escaping her lips as she watched him go. The feeling in her chest, the shame and regret that had clawed their way up from that deep, dark place inside, threatened to consume her. It was exactly how she'd felt at the hospital, realizing that she'd lost Luke's baby, the baby she'd planned to give away. The pregnancy she'd originally planned to abort. The pain was sharp, just as fresh as it had been that day.

Unable to hold in her anguish, Aubrey crawled into the tent and closed her eyes.

TWENTY

It was pitch-black outside when Luke returned, the rustle of tree branches waking Aubrey from her exhausted doze. She sat up, wiping sleep from her eyes, ready to face whatever Luke had to say. When he poked his head into the tent, the lack of anger in his expression startled her.

"Hey," he said. "Can I come in?"

"It's your tent," Aubrey said, feeling silly.

Luke climbed in, settling beside her. He reached out and took her hand.

"Aubrey, I'm so sorry," he said, stealing her breath.

"W-What?" she stuttered, confused.

"I'm sorry that any of that happened to you. I'm sorry for what happened with your ex, I'm sorry I wasn't more careful using protection, and I'm sorry that you had to make that kind of choice," he said. He squeezed her hand. "No one should have to go through that. I just… I wish you'd told me sooner. I didn't get why you were so resistant to me, when we have such good chemistry. Now I think I understand a little better."

"I'm told you the part about Lawrence because I want you to understand why I left you in San Diego without saying goodbye. I had such a perfect weekend with you, and I just wanted to keep it that way. It made me feel so good, and I wasn't ready for anything more. It was like a snow globe, like a perfect moment trapped in a bubble. I could pick it up and think about it and feel good any time I wanted. You gave me that," Aubrey said. "But I knew that if you got close to me, I'd have to tell you the rest, and then you'd leave. And I really, really… Luke, I don't want that."

Luke gave her a long, measured look. For a moment she was worried that he might still be angry, but instead he leaned in and brushed a kiss against her lips.

"I guess I never thought of it that way, like trapping a memory in a snow globe. But I did the same thing. I thought about you all the time when I was overseas, fantasized about you more than I'd like to admit. After Jordan, I knew I was too fucked up to come back to you. But I still thought about you all the time, I swear it," Luke said, the words sounding like both a confession and an assurance.

"Oh, Luke…" Aubrey sighed and tipped her face up. He kissed her again, deeper this time, but released her after a moment.

"When my father called us home and sat us down to tell us about the Alphas' decree, my brothers went nuts. They were all so angry, and rightfully so. I was pissed for a minute, getting caught up in their anger, but then... Then I realized that I might have another chance to see you. I looked for you at the mixer, even though I was sure that you would have already settled down with someone else. I know I fucked things up back there..."

"You didn't fuck anything up. I had no right to be jealous, not after I walked out on you in San Diego," Aubrey corrected him.

"Still. I should have done more. I was planning to come find you, but the whole party thing just freaked me out so bad. And then I started drinking, and that girl appeared out of nowhere..." Luke ran his free hand through his hair, giving his head a frustrated shake. "God, when I saw you, I really lost it. You were long gone by the time I was sober enough to chase you, too. I was so pissed at myself."

"And what about... the other part?" Aubrey asked him, swallowing.

"I wish you'd found me sooner, told me everything. But I can't be mad about what I couldn't seem to do myself. And the pregnancy... Aubrey, none of that is your fault. You did nothing wrong."

"I was going to have an abortion," Aubrey said, fresh tears forming in her eyes. "I was very rational about it. I made the appointment. I basically poisoned the well. I felt like… like I lost the baby because it knew it wasn't wanted."

"Aubrey," Luke said, very serious. "That's not true, and you know it. Those things just happen. If you could will a baby away, I think we'd know about it by now. I don't want you to waste your time and energy thinking stuff like that. Don't poison your own well, to use your phrase."

"So… that's it? You just forgive me?" she asked, wiping her damp cheeks with the back of her hand.

"There's nothing to forgive. In a way, it's kind of nice to be with someone with their own baggage. It makes me feel less unworthy," he said, lifting a shoulder.

Aubrey smirked, wrinkling her nose at him.

"That's sweet, in a fucked up kind of way," she said.

"I know, I know. But now… we're both here. And maybe I'm all fucked up, and maybe you're scared to take a mate, but… we just have the whole world at our fingertips, Aubrey. We can go as fast or as slow as we want, I don't care. I just want us to do it all together," he finished.

"What about Portland?" Aubrey asked.

"Screw Portland. Let's move to a cabin in the woods and never see anyone else again. I can telecommute or something," Luke declared.

"And what about my job, which I love?" Aubrey prompted.

"Aubrey Umbridge, if you'll have me, I will live anywhere you want. Honestly," Luke said, exasperated.

"What about a sea shanty? Or like, a really noisy condo in the middle of downtown?" she asked, knowing he'd hate that scenario.

"Condo, shanty. Check and check," he said with a laugh.

"Fine. Well, I guess I can't turn that offer down," she said, fluttering her eyelashes.

"That's underwhelming," Luke joked back.

Aubrey flung herself at him, pressing her body against his. She pressed her lips to his, loving how small she felt as he wrapped his arms around her.

"I want you, Luke. Right now," Aubrey whispered.

"You've got me, Aubrey," Luke promised her. "Any time of the day or night, any place."

"Take me into the tent," she sighed.

As Luke swept her up and carried her inside, Aubrey thought her heart might burst with happiness.`

Aubrey loved the tender care Luke showed as he laid her down on the tent's thick pallet bed. His movements were calm and deliberate, and Aubrey realized that she'd never once seen her mate like this, at peace with himself and the world around him.

Luke stretched out beside her, his fingers twining with hers. He gave her a long, languorous kiss, lips and tongue exploring with gentle strokes. Aubrey sucked in a deep breath, already burning for him though they were both still fully dressed. Luke had a way of doing that to her, making her want more than she'd ever thought possible.

She tugged his thin gray sweater and soft cotton shirt up, slipping her hand beneath to let her fingers play over the taut flesh there. She swept her touch upward from his waistline, her thumb dipping to trace the vee of muscle beside his hip bone. Luke's abs clenched, betraying his sensitivity to her caress even as he nipped her bottom lip, reminding her of his dominance.

Aubrey pulled back and pulled at his shirt, pleased when Luke sat up and helped her shuck it from his body.

"You really are something," she marveled, running her hands down the rippling perfection of his shoulders and arms, casting a glance at the sculpted perfection of his chest and abs.

"Look who's talking," Luke said, arching a brow.

Aubrey silenced him, kissing him hard as she pushed him onto his back. She watched his face closely as she found the button on his pants and unzipped them. The lust and adoration she saw in his eyes floored her, made her bold. In half a minute, she had him stripped down to his tight gray boxer briefs, her eyes drinking in every inch of bared skin.

Kissing him again, light and teasing this time, she trailed her fingertips over his hip bones and the tops of his thighs. His cock twitched as he gave a soft growl, a demand that she get on with it. Aubrey planned to take her sweet time and explore every inch of her man, though.

Hooking her fingers in his waist band, she pulled the boxer briefs down his hips, freeing his erection. She took it in her hand, astounded anew at his sheer size. The base of his cock was too thick for her to close her fingers around it, and when it lay against his body it nearly reached up to his navel. All shifters were big, but Luke certainly took the cake.

Luke groaned, his eyes fluttering closed as he thrust into her hand. Aubrey stroked the silky-hard flesh from crown to root, her thumb tracing the thick veins just under the skin. She swept her thumb over the blunt head, spreading the slick precum with her touch.

Tossing her long hair back over her shoulder, Aubrey leaned in and gave him a single, long lick from bottom to top before closing her lips around the crown. Luke cried out, his whole body going rigid.

Just that fast, Luke withdrew. He grabbed Aubrey and pulled her down beside him, rising to tower over her.

"No more of that," he scolded.

"But—" Aubrey started.

"It's been too long for me. I want to make this good for you, and you're about to blow it all. Literally," he told her, lips twitching with amusement.

She hmmphed, but she was too turned on to be upset. She'd get her turn to control his pleasure, even if it wasn't right this minute.

"Why am I the only one naked?" Luke asked, pretending exasperation. He peeled the dress from her body, ignoring her faint protests when he stripped off her bra and panties, too. Aubrey's lust dimmed; she felt too exposed, almost embarrassed as Luke's eyes skated over her bountiful, naked flesh.

When she tried to cover herself, her hands landing on her rounded stomach, Luke growled at her.

"Quit ruining my view," he scolded, pulling her hands away. "You're too damn beautiful, I want to kiss you everywhere but I can't decide where to start."

Aubrey blushed as Luke laid down beside her and pulled her body against his. Her breasts and thighs brushed against his body, giving her a tantalizing hint of the warmth that radiated from him. Luke brushed a kiss at the corner of her mouth, dropping kisses to her jawline and down to her neck. He nuzzled her ear, making her shiver with pleasure.

He kissed her neck and shoulders as his hands found her breasts, measuring their heavy weight. He teased her nipples with this thumbs as he marked her neck with quick nips of his teeth. Desire burned bright within her once again, her breasts aching and burning even as liquid desire pooled at her core.

"Luke…" she whispered.

He turned his attention to her breasts, brushing the light growth of his beard against the tender underside of each. When his lips closed over her nipple she moaned and arched her back, wanting more. As he laved his tongue over her nipple, his fingers traced a line down her stomach and lower, finding and exploring her lower lips.

"Fuck, you're wet for me already," Luke gritted out. He abandoned her breasts, his fingers parting her lips, circling her core.

At the first touch of his fingertips against her clit, Aubrey nearly came. Her skin felt too tight, moisture forming on her flesh as need consumed her. She wanted more, needed more, but she couldn't bring herself to stop him. His deft fingers drew her higher and higher until she thought she would shatter. Just before she peaked, she pulled back.

"What's wrong?" Luke asked, giving her a deep kiss.

"I want us to go together," Aubrey said. She hadn't spoken her desires aloud since she'd been with him in San Diego, and it felt a little uncomfortable.

Luke's answering growl, the way he grabbed her waist to pull her close and gave her a demanding kiss, told her that she'd said the right thing.

To Aubrey's surprise, Luke pulled her onto his body, settling her to straddle his hips. He bucked upward when her heat came down to cradle his cock, grinding into her. He reached up and flipped the dark curtain of her hair over her shoulder, his eyes practically glowing with lust.

"Look at you," he said again, shaping her hips with his hands, cupping her breasts. "Fuck, Aubrey. I need to be inside you."

Luke lifted her a little, grasping his erection and teasing her core with the thick tip. Aubrey shifted, aligning their bodies so that the head of his cock pressed into the entrance of her slick, needy channel.

Inch by agonizing inch, Aubrey took him in, shivering as her body stretched to accommodate his size.

Luke gripped her hips, a tortured expression on his face, but to his credit he didn't do more than hiss out a long breath.

"Fuck me, Aubrey. You feel so good, better than I remembered," he said. A vein throbbed at his temple, more standing out in his thickly muscled arms as he kept himself tightly reined.

The second that Aubrey started to move, he moved with her. She raised and lowered herself, the feel of his cock rubbing in every sensitive spot making goosebumps prickle her flesh.

Luke was still restrained, distracting himself by kneading and kissing her breasts as she set a slow, deep rhythm. Waves of liquid heat rippled up through her body as she increased her pace, her breasts bouncing and ass landing against Luke with a satisfying slap.

Still he waited; her mate had the patience of a saint. Aubrey wanted none of it, though.

"Fuck me, Luke. Let go," she ordered.

Luke thrust up into her body, filling her completely, and they both groaned with satisfaction. He moved under her, his hands clenching her ample hips once more as they found a rough, fevered tempo. Luke's blue-green gaze was intent on her face, and Aubrey couldn't stop watching him.

All Luke's careful control disappeared as he pounded into her body, emitting pleased growls with every flick of Aubrey's hips.

"You're so tight, so hot," he ground out. "I can't wait…"

His broad thumb found her clit, rubbing it in insistent circles until her body tightened, tensing as she reached the peak. Luke's mouth found the sensitive curve of her breast, his teeth sinking into her flesh, creating a bright burst of pleasure and pain that shattered her in an instant.

Aubrey shouted her release as her body clenched and clamped around Luke's cock, the sensation so intense that for a moment she knew nothing but stars bursting in darkness. Luke's matching cry pulled her back and Aubrey cried out again as he rocked into her body, pulsing his seed deep into her womb. His cock jerked over and over again, the joy of ecstasy and release plain on his face.

When he slowed, dragging in desperate breaths, Luke grabbed the back of Aubrey's neck and pulled her roughly down, pressing her to his chest. They lay joined for minutes, or hours, or forever, breathing each other in as their hearts thundered in their chests. Aubrey tucked her face against Luke's sweat dampened neck, taking a deep draw of his masculine scent into her lungs.

At last Luke shifted underneath her, and Aubrey knew she had to move so that he could breathe. She had to be crushing him, no matter how big he might be. When she started to pull away, Luke grabbed her neck again, a possessive gesture that made her stomach flip flop.

"Where are you going?" he asked, his other hand cupping her ass before slipping up to rub lazy circles on her back.

"I was just—"

"Don't move on my account. I'd keep you right here forever if I could," Luke sighed, nuzzling her ear and kissing her neck until she giggled.

"I'm just… you know, getting comfortable," Aubrey said, rolling over to lay beside him. "You're about a thousand degrees, you know."

"And whose fault is that?" Luke teased, kissing her. "You got me all riled up. God, my bear is even more in love with you than I am."

Aubrey froze. Could he possibly mean that?

"Hey," Luke said, tilting her chin up so that he could see her face.

"Yeah," Aubrey said, giving him a halfhearted smile.

"Seriously. You have to know that I love you, right?"

"Luke, you don't have to—"

"Hold that thought. Don't move," he told her. He sat up and looked around, grabbing his clothes and rifling through his pants pockets.

Aubrey frowned at him, already missing the body heat she'd so recently mocked. When he laid back down, facing her, she felt content again. She smiled up at him, ready to snuggle closer and drift off to sleep.

"Wait, wait. I know I wore you out, but give me a

second here," Luke said. He took her hand and opened it, pressing a small object into her palm. Aubrey held it up in front of her face, blinking.

"A ring box," she said aloud, feeling dumb.

"Uh, yeah." Luke gave her a look, reaching over and opening the box. Inside lay a dazzling diamond and sapphire ring, more bling than Aubrey had ever held in her hand.

"Luke!" she cried. She smacked his chest with her free hand, confused. "What the hell?"

"Look. You don't have to wear it. Maybe you think it's ugly," he started.

"No! No. It's beyond beautiful," Aubrey said, tears welling in her eyes.

"I just… You know, I want you to be my mate, and I want you to wear my ring. Am I fucking this up?" he asked, noticing the tears that started to roll down Aubrey's cheeks.

"No," she said, her voice going hoarse.

"Aubrey Rose Umbridge, you… you're it for me," Luke said. "Will you please wear my beyond beautiful ring?"

"Y-yes?" Aubrey said, stunned.

Luke looked at her for a long moment and then grinned.

"I'll take what I can get," he joked. He took the ring box and pulled the ring free. When he slipped it onto her finger, Aubrey couldn't hold back a sob. "Seriously though, please tell me these are happy tears. Please."

"I love you, too," Aubrey blurted out, throwing her arms around Luke. He laughed, giving her a squeeze.

"Thank fucking god," he said, pulling back to give her a kiss. "Now that was worth delaying your bedtime, I hope?"

Aubrey smacked his chest again, then held out her hand to admire the ring.

"Mates," she said aloud.

"Mates," Luke echoed, taking her hand and pulling her close.

Though it was the last thing in the world Aubrey had expected out of her day.. hell, her whole life to date, she couldn't remember a moment she'd been happier. Not even back in San Diego, where it all begun.

TO BE CONTINUED...

Not so fast! These white-hot Alpha bears have only just begun to thrill you. Noah's Revelation, the second full-length book in the Red Lodge Bears series, available now on Amazon! **Turn to the next page for a glimpse of Noah and Charlotte's story.**

Charlotte was always a good girl, always a dutiful daughter, a benevolent nurse. In this moment, though, she saw herself reflected in Noah and Finn's gazes: a sexy bombshell, something they wanted to pleasure and devour. She wanted that, she wanted it so badly it nearly hurt. It had been over a year since her last one-night-stand, and suddenly she didn't want to wait another minute. She was tipsy and horny and ready, ready for the promises she saw written on Noah and Finn's faces.

Only… how was she supposed to choose between them? They were literally identically handsome, though she was fond of Noah's longer hair. She reached up and thrust her fingers into his damp, disheveled locks, loving how warm and soft his hair felt against her fingers. She could imagine herself tugging at those locks while he did unimaginably dirty things to her…

Then she looked up at Finn, thinking how caring and kind he was. He was all the things she looked for in a man, all the things she'd never found in such a pretty package before. He'd be a careful, thorough lover, taking care of her every want.

Finn wore a light gray dress shirt and a black tie with dark slacks, where Noah was dressed once again in a white shirt and black dress pants. Noah's shirt was unbuttoned at the collar, giving her a glimpse of smooth, tan skin. Finn cut such a dashing figure in his tie, though…

She looked between the two one last time and heaved a sigh. She arched her back, bringing her lips to Finn's ear.

"How am I supposed to choose one of you?" she asked, her tone pleading.

Finn stiffened against her, and she noticed that Noah mirrored him after a second. She raised her head and looked at Noah, who was engaging in some silent communication with Finn. For a moment, Charlotte actually wondered if they had some kind of twin telepathy. She giggled to herself, her lips twisting up in a smile.

Noah lowered his lips to her ear, his warm breath against her sensitive flesh making her shiver.

"You don't have to choose tonight, Charlotte. Do you want us both?" he asked.

Charlotte bit her lip, looking up at him. His expression was sincere, free of judgment. She nodded, and was rewarded when Noah brushed his lips against her neck. Half a second later, Finn kissed her neck in the same spot on the other side, and Charlotte thought she might die from want.

ABOUT THE AUTHOR

Kayla Gabriel lives in the wilds of Minnesota where she swears she sees shifters in the woods beyond her yard. Her favorite things in life are mini marshmallows, coffee and when people use their blinker.

Connect with Kayla by
email: kaylagabrielauthor@gmail.com and be sure to
get her FREE book: freeshifterromance.com

http://kaylagabriel.com